GLIMPSES

OF

FORGOTTEN

DREAMS

***

GLIMPSES

OF

FORGOTTEN

DREAMS

a novel by

DANIEL HILL ZAFREN

TIME TREASURES

Published by Time Treasures Books, West Jefferson, North Carolina

ISBN 13: 978-0-9778892-8-0

Printed in the United States of America

Cover and interior design by Susan Newman Design, Inc.

Earlier noteworthy books by the author, Daniel Hill Zafren:

In a World We Never Made (2001)
A Door Never Opened (2003)
Shadow Selves (2005)
Network of Death (2006)
Not Lost — Just Not Found (2008)
Restless Beauty (2009)

www.timetreasuresbooks.com

Moreover, something is or seems
That touches me with mystic gleams
      Like glimpses of forgotten dreams —

The Two Voices
Alfred Lord Tennyson

And falling on my weary brain,
      Like a fast-falling shower,
The dreams of youth came back again, —
Low lispings of the summer rain,
Dropping on the golden grain,
      As once upon the flower.

Visions of childhood! Stay, oh, stay!
      Ye were so sweet and wild!
And distant voices seemed to say,
"It cannot be! They pass away!
Other themes demand thy lay;
      Thou are no more a child!

Prelude – Voices of the Night
Henry Wadsworth Longfellow

***

ONE

"Who says you can't take it with you?"

After uttering that common philosophical question, he pulled out a tattered picture postcard from the inside pocket of his sports jacket. He showed the picture to the five people at his luncheon table, and the laughter was boisterous. The picture showed a moving van unloading its contents in a cemetery.

Seventy-eight year old Stanley Veritan had been in *Mountain Splendor* retirement home for only three months, and he had a reputation right from the day he moved there of being a jokester. His failing body was a poor companion for his quick mind. Puns and funny stories abounded. Once he sensed that this was what these people expected, wanted and needed from him, the delivery was right on cue. The only problem was that such was not his true nature. For him to be a comedian took great effort.

At the completion of lunch, most of the inhabitants of the home went to their rooms for a nap or other quiet time, as the numerous activities offered by the staff did not begin until later in the afternoon. Stanley chose, as was his discovery, to sit on the bench on the far perimeter of the grounds where the view of the mountains was unobstructed. There he could engage in the personal activity that had sustained him all of his life. His thought processes would reign supreme, and his overactive mind, which had not slowed in his advanced years, projected him through the past, the present, and the future with incredible fluidity. He was sure that because of this mental acumen even his dreams were clear and amazingly real. He even caught glimpses of forgotten dreams. Thus, he felt he had already lived his life twice as long as most people. He was functioning mentally at full tilt twenty-four hours a day. He had even joked to himself that after he died he should will his brain to the Smithsonian Institution. But, that was the limit of his personal humor. If his mind ever did abandon him, he might just as well be dead.

He was serious as a child, perhaps overly serious. Rather than accept things that transpired around him, a deep analysis of the situations would precede any action on his part. Other children shunned association with him often branding him as no fun to be with. Through the course of that youthful development he did not laugh or smile unless there was a good reason to do so. He lost himself in the world of books to placate his studious inclination and where being glum was totally immaterial.

Stanley's parents were constantly frustrated with him as all they could do was to classify his withdrawn nature as a form of unreasonable stubbornness. Their attention shifted more to Stanley's brother and sister never quite referred to, but surely deemed, as more normal. The parents' sigh of relief came when they sent Stanley off to a small teacher's college more than a thousand miles away.

It was in this college that Stanley's character fully blossomed and was constantly being refined. He lived off-campus in a small basement apartment, and from that isolated nest he would pick and choose whom he would associate with and what at the school he would participate in.

In his second year, he met Cindy, his Cinderella. A chance meeting at a poetry reading, and within a few moments they knew they were kindred spirits. Completely ethereal and book enhanced, her parents also did not understand her behavior and as an act of relief shipped her off to the college. Also a sophomore, they often wondered why they had not met that entire first year. It mattered not. Their pasts and personalities afforded a unity that was fast and permanent.

A year later they eloped. Their respective families did not even blink. They accepted such an action as the typical errant behavior they had long endured.

They lived together in the basement apartment, taking odd jobs to sustain their lives. The parents, at least, continued to pay their tuition, perhaps fearing that if they did not the offbeat couple would live with them. They studied together, and spent extensive hours reading. Long walks, hand-in-hand, prompted intricate discussions and plans for a togetherness that was as natural to them as the steps they took on the pathways through and around the college.

After graduation, they were able to find teaching positions at the same elementary school in a small town in Connecticut. Their easy-going mannerisms and abundant book knowledge constantly endeared them to the children and entertained them with sparks to the imagination that delighted the little ones. After finding a sea captain's jacket and hat in an antique shop that fit him perfectly, Stanley took the attire to the school and kept it in the wardrobe. Whenever he would go to the wardrobe and don the jacket and the hat, the children would squeal with delight knowing they were about to embark on a literary adventure far and wide.

Stanley and Cindy became the most popular teachers at the school, and after forty years they retired. Former students, from artists to wealthy businesspersons, flooded in from all parts of the nation when the joint retirement celebration took place. After all, because of the Veritans distant horizons were opened up for exploring and the quests undertaken were challenges to be conquered. A host of former students spoke paying tribute to the duo for nourishing a love for books, giving imagination wings, and instilling a firm and confident belief in abilities.

For this entire period, they lived in a small stone house deep in the woods. Surrounded by the beauty of nature and the solitude of the hideaway, a deep and abiding love sustained them. When Cindy died three years after retirement, Stanley was constantly comforted by the memory of the long and full years they had spent together.

They brought a son into the world, Thomas. As hard as they tried to guide and nourish him in the happy ways of their existence, Thomas was a social rebel. He resented being stuck far in the woods, and he thirsted for freedom and independence. Eventually, Thomas became a successful corporate manager and settled in Chicago with his wife, a cold and hard woman from a prominent social family. Visits were few and unfulfilling for all, contacts strained, and two grandchildren were probably indoctrinated about the strange grandparents.

When Stanley's health started its unwarranted decline, and he was unable to shift for himself at his home, it was a foregone conclusion that Thomas and family would not welcome Stanley into their home. With the son's prosperity, he could easily afford to place his peculiar father in this retirement home in the mountains of Vermont. It was far enough away to avoid visits, and yet was to be a comfortable place where conscience need never be faced directly.

A short and sad story when all is said and done. Unfortunately, a plight echoed throughout the retirement home by so many of the residents. Lives are compartmentalized, and as soon as the new aspect of a life is entered where apparent uselessness seems pervasive, body and mind are cast aside to wither and die. Being provided for is surely an empty gesture when unaccompanied by love, respect and compassion. No less a person because of age and infirmity, the elderly are forced to exist in that preordained mode until death becomes a welcome relief. Old mouths can speak but young ears do not want to listen. Society turns its back on a valuable asset, those who are tried and true. The humorist, Art Linkletter, put it this way: *The four steps of men are infancy, childhood, adolescence, and obsolescence.* Wisdom and maturity are to lay fallow and an old person is forced to face death as a form of punishment. Even in many hospitals, the elderly do not receive the same care as younger persons. After all, they are to die soon anyway.

At these bench-sitting sessions, he talked with his Cindy, at least to her permanency in his soul. He derived great comfort in these solitary monologues. He just knew she was nodding in agreement at his observations and conclusions. At such meaningful moments, he was true to himself and to her. Therein lay the value and substance of his existence.

Rooms at the home were assigned in the independent living wing by seniority of length of residence. The long ensconced folks had the rooms in the front of the building with a view of trees and the mountains. Newer residents had rooms in the back with a look only out at the visitor's parking lot and some small local business complexes beyond that.

Stanley looked around his room, and he longed for the home where he and Cindy had the accumulated possessions of their life of love. Here, he had only a handful of special books, photographs and meaningful small antiques that they had acquired during many drives through the countryside stopping at any antique shop that was open. Thomas had everything else sold at auction before he put the house on the market for sale. As part of the entry requirements to the home, Stanley had to give a power of attorney to Thomas.

Stanley did not know how much longer his life would last. Doctors were treating him for an assortment of maladies, and none were optimistic about recovery and longevity. Stanley did not fear dying, grateful that he had a relatively long and happy life. For all of their so-called normal attributes, his brother and sister had died some years earlier. He was never close to them, and they never made any overtures to change that. He was sure they had picked up on the distancing overtly displayed by his parents. They, too, had died years ago. So, in reality, in his closing days, he had no one.

One of the meaningful games that he and Cindy engaged in was to copy passages or cut out items from sorted sources that caught their fancy from their readings and to put them in a silver box. It did not take long for that box to be jammed full. They bought a small antique trunk at a shop they stumbled on, and the excerpts were housed in what they then referred to as their treasure chest. The treasure chest was with him now, and he would find relaxation and stimulation in plucking a tidbit out, recalling when it was excised from a larger work, and then reading it aloud so that Cindy might share in the delight. The sea captain's hat was also housed in there, and he would put it on whenever he read a choice from the contents. At times he would go to the closet and pull out the captain's jacket. It was quite worn and his expanded girth would not allow him to button it up. Nevertheless he would put it on to complete his uniform. He opened the treasure chest, recalling a poem that he associated with Cindy when he read it. It was near the top of the heap and easy to locate.

> *As a twig trembles, which a bird*
> > *Lights on to sing, then leaves unbent,*
> *So is my memory thrilled and stirred, —*
> > *I only know she came and went.*

> *Oh, when the room grows slowly dim.*
> > *And life's last oil is nearly spent,*
> *One gush of light these eyes will brim,*
> > *Only to think she came and went.*

> She Came and Went
> James Russell Lowell

Now in the nostalgic mood, he remembered a favorite description by Robert Browning that ably summed up his present situation. It took somewhat of a hunt to find it, but he was rewarded by its recovery.

> *Well, onward though alone! Small time re-*
> > *mains,*
> *And much to do: I must have fruit, must reap*
> *Some profit from my toils. I doubt my body*
> *Will hardly serve me through; while I have la-*
> > *bored*
> *It has decayed; and now that I demand*
> *Its best assistance, it will crumble fast:*
> *A sad thought, a sad fate! How very full*
> *Of wormwood 't is, that just at alter-service,*
> *The rapt hymn rising with the rolling smoke,*
> *When glory dawns and all is at the best,*
> *The sacred fire may flicker and grow faint*
> *And die for want of a wood-piler's help!*
> *Thus fades the flagging body, and the soul*
> *Is pulled down in the overthrow. Well, well —*

Let men catch every word. Let them lose naught
Of what I say; something may yet be done.

     He took his pills and headed for the dining room where he would sit at a different table with other residents so that he might lift their spirits with comical stories. Many of these stories emerged from the vast storehouse of his readings over a lifetime. Many were now housed in the treasure chest. Often, he would embellish them or alter the venue or personalities in the story to make it more germane for the listening group. He had done the same with the children in his classes over a teaching lifetime. Secretly, he would wish for a quick meal so that he could retreat to his room.

     Back in the room, he would sit in the arm chair and raise his feet on the ottoman. His mind vividly alive would lead him from thought to thought, as this was the vitality connecting him to Cindy, to his being. The thoughts would vary from expansive observations of the world to more intimate mental images of his dreams both lived and anticipated despite his doctors' dire diagnosis. Each thought was a mental adventure. The thoughts would be so close, so life-like, so endearing, he felt he could just easily reach out and touch them.

TWO

For old and tired eyes, it was mesmerizing staring out of the windshield to the snow-covered road. Snow was still falling, and the sound of the windshield wipers echoed her faint heart beat. Lauren Chastner glanced sideways at Penny who was intently staring ahead to guide the car carefully over the slippery road. Lauren felt sorry for her niece, knowing full well she did not want to put her ailing spinster aunt in a nursing home. Yet, Lauren agreed to accept that alternative so that the young woman might have a life of her own with some semblance of peace.

Lauren, now seventy-seven, and failing daily could no longer stay in her small Boston apartment. Going from a place that was home for fifty years would leave a scar in her heart for whatever short time she had left. The doctors agreed she was terminally ill but they were not sure how much longer she might have left. Her energy was sapped and there was little left for her senses to react to. Yet, her mind was intact and she took great pride and satisfaction that she was doing this for her niece. Her only sister's child was her sole relative. Her sister had passed away six years ago. Penny was a drug company representative and traveled extensively. She made good money but would be unable to care for her aunt, as much as she wanted to. Lauren knew this and wanted to spare the good natured and kind-hearted woman from the dilemma of trying to do the impossible.

Lauren forfeited her life savings to be accepted into *Mountain Splendor*. Penny would also provide some supplemental payments when the cost rose, as Lauren might be shifted from independent living quarters to the assisted living feature as dependence arose. The home had a fine reputation due to the full range of services it could provide. As a rural facility it was more cost effective.

Actually, a country place would be quite a change for Lauren. Being a teacher in the Boston school system for nearly fifty years and living all of that time in a large city, her exposure to any profusion of nature was limited. She had never married. Pinched lips and a gaunt face with thick glasses atop an underdeveloped female body led to no serious romantic involvements. Long ago, she had resigned herself to a life alone, but she had never felt lonely. The children in her classes were her family, and as an avid reader her books were her constant and ingratiating companions.

She had been close to her sister, and was delighted to be an aunt when Penny was born. Her sister was divorced soon after that birth and never remarried. Yet, she lived near to Lauren and maintained a warm and loving home for her daughter. Especially on holidays and birthdays Lauren was able to share in that comforting environment. When her mother died, Penny always tried to include Lauren in many aspects of her busy life. Being grateful for the smallest of efforts was one of the keys to Lauren's humanity.

When they reached the home, Lauren encouraged Penny to start back before the weather turned any worse. She gave her niece the strongest embrace she was capable of, and as she watched her drive off the last vestige of her former life left with her. As she watched Penny's car pull out into the thickening snow, she recalled being with her sister at Penny's fifth birthday. Penny asked her mother why she was named Penny. Her mother thought for a moment and in the same soft and loving tone she used constantly, she responded, "So that others would not know that you are worth millions of dollars and try to steal you away from me. Having you makes me the richest person in the world."

The resident administrator of the home, Carol Seton, was friendly and explained everything patiently to Lauren. She showed her to her room at the back of the building and had one of the staff bring the bags to the room. Nobody else seemed to be around, and Carol explained that all were in their rooms preparing for dinner, which was a little more than an hour away. Carol said she would be back to take her to the dining room and get her introduced.

Left by her, Lauren noted that the room was clean and cheerful, even though the bed, dresser, armchair and tiny desk took up much of the space. A small bathroom was off to the side. The snow was falling heavily now and being blown around by gusty winds so she could not see much from the window.

She felt tired and sat on the bed. She would do the unpacking later. There was little doubt that this was a new phase of her life. It seemed incongruous that the last phase of her life would be a new one. Whatever it turned out to be, she would be her own person to the end. She never let anyone get a glimpse of her weaknesses, and these would go with her to the grave. She had a satisfying life even if the shining moments and accomplishments were not shared intimately with another. One can be strong alone. Physical weakness and infirmity would not detract from her acute thinking and emotional stability. She would not let anything intrude on that nucleus of the person she had been. Only death would end her life as she defined it.

When Carol came by, Lauren asked if she could get a little bookcase as some books were going to be shipped there. It would be a squeeze but Carol thought it could be arranged.

It looked as if all of the residents were in the dining room when they got there. Meals were the prime occupation of each day and an important social event. In the dining room, there were twelve tables with five or six settings at each table. Two waitresses, in uniform, served all. Unless one was on a special dietary plan, there was no menu and all were served the same food. The residents in the other wings of the building in various degrees of assisted living had the food brought to them in their rooms. The great majority of the occupants of the tables were women, and as Lauren scanned the room the limited number of men were dispersed to various tables.

Carol took Lauren to the front where there was a microphone. "Sorry to interrupt, but we have a new arrival. Please welcome Lauren Chastner and introduce yourselves when you can. Lauren, we are happy to have you in our family."

Carol led Lauren to a table on the side where four women and a man were sitting. Carol thought it would be less awkward to put Carol at a table where Stanley was sitting as his stories would put the woman at ease and she would not have to force herself to make conversation with people she was just meeting.

Lauren looked across the table at Stanley, and what she saw was an old man as frail as she was. Yet, he still had a full head of thick brown hair that was barely streaked with gray. Her own thinning hair had turned gray when she was quite a bit younger. Even with her poor eyesight, she was sure she noted a glimmer in the sunken eyes. What she especially found appealing was his calm and soothing voice. His diction was perfect, and she could very much appreciate that.

The other ladies at the table were pressing him for a story. He put his fork down in a dramatic fashion. "Alright. One story and then you must let me chew my food while I have any energy left." He looked from face to face around the table sure that he had eye contact with the entire assembly. "In medieval times, a harsh king was sitting on his throne with the queen on a throne beside him. He summoned the court jester. 'Jester, I want you to give me an example of where an explanation is worse than the deed itself. You have until sunrise to come up with one. If you don't, off with your head.' With that said, he rose and took the queen's hand as they headed for their chambers. The jester came up behind them and pinched the king on his bottom. The king turned around furiously and said, 'Why did you do that?'

9

To this, the jester replied, 'Oops, I'm sorry. I thought you were the queen.'"

The ladies laughed heartily, and Lauren could not help but smile. Pinched lips are not the true revelation of the breadth of a smile. She did enjoy the story and marveled at the aged storyteller.

After dinner, as was his custom, Stanley stole off to his room. Each day was a long day and he thirsted more than ever for the quiet time to be with his close personal thoughts.

Many of the residents went to the lounge to watch television. Lauren passed by the lounge on the way to her room. She took a quick look in and noted that Stanley was not there. Once in the room, she unpacked her bags. She turned down the blanket and smelled the clean sheets. The housekeeping staff was in charge of cleaning the rooms and making the beds each day. Lauren doubted she was up to doing any of that.

As she lay down in the bed, one thought flickered in her mind before sleep overtook the weak body. *If the court jester pinched her, what sort of explanation would he offer?*

THREE

Breakfast at *Mountain Splendor* was handled differently. Instead of a set time and menu as with the other meals, breakfast was served from 7:00 to 9:00 with a choice of limited morning-type foods. The social draw was not as evident as with the other meals, and more than half of the residents would not even show up, preferring to sleep late and hold off until lunch.

Stanley had always been an early riser, another by-product of a mind in high gear. He and Cindy would get up before sunrise, have a first cup of coffee, and then take a walk through the woods as the sun crept up over the horizon. They would return to the house and have another cup of coffee with cereal and a muffin. At an early age, they took Thomas with them but he showed no enthusiasm about it and at school age adamantly refused to go. He would wait at the house for one of them to drive him to the school bus stop two miles down the road.

At 7:00 Stanley was waiting at the dining room door for the staff to open up. He was usually the only one there, and once inside he would relax with a bowl of oatmeal with brown sugar and two cups of coffee. The doctors frowned on him having coffee, but it was an ingrained vice to launch the day, a coveted morning ritual. It was also a bridge to his loving and sharing past, a bridge he could not and would not dismantle. This morning, he had company to wait for the dining room to open. He watched Lauren move slowly down the hall, and she smiled slightly as she approached him.

Lauren had also always been an early riser. The newspaper would be delivered outside of her apartment door, and she would read it while she had coffee and a Danish or other pastry that she would have gotten the day before at the wonderful small bakery down the street. She would stop there on her way home from school. She could remember the wonderful smells of the freshly baked goods. The baker would cut a wedge from a large raisin pumpernickel bread that usually sat upon the counter for Lauren to sample as she chose her daily pastry. There can be such simple pleasures in life, and she always tried to recognize and appreciate them as such.

"Good morning, Stanley."

"Top of the day to you, Lauren."

"They're not open yet, I see."

"It usually takes them a few minutes after seven to realize I am here. You would think they would know by now, since this is my morning appointed time."

Lauren wanted to say something witty, believing he would appreciate that. Actually, she could think of nothing to say. That was a relief to Stanley, torn between wanting to be alone and sensing he should be friendly to a newcomer, especially one who appeared to be in a similarly poor physical condition.

A waitress opened the door and they entered. Only two tables were set up. Without speaking, they sat next to each other. Stanley had his usual, and Lauren ordered coffee and an English muffin. As if each respected the other's quiet time, no words were exchanged. It might have appeared awkward to an outside observer, yet each was at peace and apparently respectful of the other's solitude.

As they finished, Stanley glanced at this woman and took note of her proud bearing in spite of such apparent failing health. It was a mirror image of him. "There is probably two feet of snow out there. When the weather is hospitable, I take a walk outside after breakfast. I have the grounds to myself. By the time I get back, the newspapers have been delivered to the front desk. Then, I retire to my room, read the paper and lose myself in thoughts only an old man has."

Her voice was weak but cultured. "An old woman can have special thoughts as well."

"That was a poor conclusion on my part, forgive me. I should have said thoughts that only an old person can have."

"Oh, I think people of all ages can have deep thoughts. It may only be old folks who can dwell on them with keen insight and can appreciate their limits or absence of limitations."

Inwardly, both had reached the same conclusion. "Here is a person I can and want to talk with."

"Since the weather will not be conducive to an outside stroll, would you care to join me for a jaunt up and down the hallway?"

She nodded. Off they went, a slow stride in unison dictated by bodies defiant to react to instant commands.

Over the next forty minutes they talked effortlessly. There was satisfaction in their mutual teaching backgrounds, and the discussions ranged from operation of the home to individual philosophies. Lauren would have guessed there would have been some funny remarks on his part, and she was glad he was more serious than her first impression of him.

Despite the bad weather, the newspapers were at the front desk. Since each copy was a special order, Lauren would have to get on the list for future deliveries. Stanley offered to bring his to her room when he was finished. It turned out to be a short trip as she was in the room next to his.

After he took the paper to her, he settled into the chair in his room staring out at the snow. He could remember the snow at the house, and he and Cindy would admire the winter wonderland. They would bundle up and trudge through the fresh snow leaving their footprints as a sign of their togetherness. It made the warmth of their love more pronounced. Animal tracks were intriguing as they tried to guess what creatures shared their woods. Talking with Lauren was reminiscent of talks with Cindy, and he was glad that the newcomer was intellectually conversant. Sharp minds bode good company.

Lauren really had no one to compare Stanley to. This had probably been the longest idea-exchange she ever had with anyone. It was exhilarating. She would have thought that it would have been intimidating but it was certainly not that. She enjoyed listening to his ideas and found it mentally challenging to respond to his openings and to formulate statements that offered him an opportunity to agree or disagree. As the half-read newspaper lay across her lap, for the moment she forgot about her ailments and felt uplifted. It is a form of magic when the mind can overpower the body so the illusion, no matter how brief, and one can feel completely young.

The telephone rang, and Lauren was startled. The noise not only surprised her, but she had not even realized that there was a telephone in the room. It was Penny inquiring how she was doing. Lauren responded that she was fine and blurted out that she had made a friend. She did not mention that it was a man. Lauren was not quite sure why she did not mention that. Perhaps, it was a continuation of the youthful feeling, a flight of fancy. Maybe, it was a personal matter. Never having a male friend, the telling about it might take an edge off its significance. If the friendship were for real, Penny would be told soon enough.

At lunch, Carol put Lauren at a different table than the one Stanley was at. There were no men at this table, and the ladies were cordial enough but Lauren was strained to make even casual conversation.

After lunch, she went back to her room, took her pills and fell asleep. Her body was dictating more to her existence, and it was becoming demanding. Any glimmer of youth dwindled in the face of reality. As long as she was mobile and could dress and feed herself, the criteria of the home for staying in the independent wing was met.

Stanley also took a nap after lunch. He was so tired these days. He would linger on one of his favorite dreams. He would be in bed with

Cindy and holding her close, their bodies fitting together as by the hand of a sculptor. The scent and warmth of her body was so real that he knew no greater satisfaction. Just as he might touch a thought, he could hold on to a memory.

FOUR

Shortly before seven the following day, Stanley knocked softly on Lauren's door. At times, drawing a breath was a hardship, tinged with pain. Yet, wanting Lauren to accompany him to breakfast was something he wanted to do and pain would not stand in the way of his wants. It was a natural desire, as if they had been doing this for a long time. It was the same for her as she was already dressed and smiled at him as they began the slow walk to the dining room. It was the start of a daily ritual, along with walks afterwards whether inside or outside of the facility. They were together at all meals, sitting side-by-side.

Nursing homes, retirement homes, or whatever else they may be called, are in effect small towns. Everyone is observed, everything is noted, and all are discussed as news items that spread rapidly among the inhabitants. It did not take long for all to know that Stanley and Lauren were close knit, if not more. Such was not graciously accepted by all. Some of the women were disturbed and some annoyed that Stanley's previously humorous demeanor had drastically been altered to a quiet and serious state. The two would talk between each other at the table and the others might just as well not be there.

Carol Seton was torn about what to do with the budding relationship. Basically, she thought it was cute for two elderly persons to be attracted to one another. She also knew that such can have distinct medical benefits when emotions are crystallized. If nothing else, it enhances the will to live. Yet, the last thing she wanted was to have to field a series of complaints from other residents and attempt to placate expressed dissatisfactions. There had been varying degrees of romances at the home before, but they had been between younger and healthier men and women. They also had not become the keen topic so quickly at the home. Torn between ignoring it and addressing it in some way, she decided to take an indirect approach and would talk to Lauren's niece about it. Penny was due to come for a visit on Saturday.

While she tried to dismiss it, Carol had a personal bias. As the resident director of the home, she had to forego any personal life of her own, including any romantic involvements. She loved her job, and felt a closeness to and was devoted to many of the residents. The one-day off a week brought little motivation to leave the place. The concern for the people could not be turned off as a spigot.

It had been a natural course for her to take this professional road. Her childhood had not been an ordinary one, and she could not recall ever actually being a child. When she was four, her parents were killed in a massive car wreck. She was raised by her father's parents. The grandparents were kindly but quite elderly. All they could do for her was to provide the necessary physical sustenance. She, in turn, had to care for them as their health hit a downward spiral. She had to rush home from school, and then cook and clean and be a concentrated caretaker for the barely able to move old ones. While robbing her of youthful adventures, it did supply her with a keen insight into the needs and views of seniors. She loved her grandparents and never begrudged the time and effort needed to provide them with some degree of care and comfort. The vitality and expanse of her teenage years were consumed in the tasks before her. At twenty, the grandparents died three months apart. She cradled each in her arms as the last breath left their weak bodies. That empathy was totally ingrained in her existence. A sensitive and caring person has many heartaches.

Carol worked and studied, finally obtaining an advanced degree in nursing home administration. Even after being hired here, a place she felt destined to be at, she kept reading and studying about the chosen field. By knowing as much as possible to do her job better, it was also a way of filling her personal loneliness. Others depended on her, and she would not let them down.

Stanley had become one of her favorites, although she attempted to treat all the residents the same. He was intelligent, outgoing and attentive, and she was drawn to him for entertainment. She was very worried about him physically, and each time she would watch from her window when he made that walk to the outer perimeter of the grounds, his movement was apparently arduous and painful. More than once she had to refrain from rushing outside to bolster him. She admired his determination. When all was said and done, she too was a bit jealous of Lauren. Not that she had any romantic interest in Stanley. She likened him to a father, a romantic intellect who captured and nourished her inner self. She did not want to be deprived of any of his attention and conversation.

The irony of it all was that Stanley and Lauren did not feel that they were a couple in a romantic sense. It had become an instantly rewarding friendship. Being in this small community, there was no way they could distance themselves from the finger pointing and gossiping.

The wind was brisk the chilly morning they braved the weather to walk outside after breakfast. He pressed her to walk to the bench that he had occupied in fairer moments. Sitting there, they huddled together for warmth.

"This is a lovely spot," Lauren spoke softly as if someone might be eavesdropping. She was as entranced with the vapor coming from her mouth as she was with the beauty of the place.

"I wanted to share it with you. It will be much more enjoyable in warmer weather, but since we have no guarantee we will be here then I just did not want an opportunity to slip by for us to be together like this."

"I am glad you have. Strange how I never had time or the inclination to appreciate the intricate beauty of nature."

"I cannot be without it. Nature represents constancy, a continuity of the cycles of life and beauty. It comforts me to know that after I am gone, such will be here for others to appreciate it."

She thought he was going to say more, but he grew quiet and pensive. She could only guess that he was thinking about his Cindy. She put her gloved hand on the arm of his coat. It was their first physical contact, albeit impeded by layers of garments. He put his glove-covered hand over her hand that was on his arm and she sensed the pressure of his fingers. They were silent for a few minutes.

"If you are cold, we can start back," he said with a hint of concern.

"In a few moments. I am enthralled with this spot and your company."

"I suppose we should decide how we should respond to the rumors."

She smiled and peered deep into his eyes. "And give credence to their wild imaginations?"

"So, you think we should do nothing to dignify any undue assertions?"

"I know enough about human nature even though I know little about Mother Nature. It would not change any minds or opinions. Any explanations or denials would merely give added fuel to the fire."

He nodded and did not say anything for a moment. "I am not sure they are entirely wrong."

"What do you mean?"

"It is a feeling, a luxury old folks have despite societal opinion to the opposite. From the start our minds shared a closeness, and it has become quite pleasurable for me."

"For me as well."

"My Cindy and I had that, and when I look back on it such was a vital component of our love. Dreams lived and dreams forgotten. Hope and belief are the children of dreams. In that sense, I believe I love you and hope you love me."

"Now that you put it that way, I think it is reasonable. As you know, I never had a great love in my life as you have had. I have no way of making any comparisons. I do know that I have a warm glow in my heart being with you and in the anticipation of just being with you. I would like to believe that such is love for me. For the short time that I have left, I would not want to be deprived of this. I recall a German proverb: The old one who is loved, is winter with flowers. I have never been a fighter perhaps because I really never had anything to fight for. I would fight anyone or anything that seeks to keep us apart."

"Lauren, I do believe you have a teenager's spunk. I admire that kind of gumption. You're truly my kind of woman."

"Spunk too late, I am afraid. Yet, if it is spunk, maybe we should give them a really good reason to talk."

He smiled broadly as he gently pulled her to a standing position and they started to walk in the direction of the building. "I second your motion for that plan of action."

As they headed back, the pact they made was not to try to avoid the whispers and the innuendoes. In fact, they would pretend to be true lovers and go out of their way to give everyone something to talk about. They would be the active thespians in their love play, the scenes to be written as they went along. An impromptu game they navigate through as they might wish.

Cold and weary from the walk, it was the day that Stanley introduced Lauren to the treasure chest. He never did think that he would share it with anyone but Cindy. Yet, it just seemed like the thing to do, knowing that Lauren would appreciate it for what it is and sensing that Cindy would understand. In effect, he was sharing himself and Cindy with Lauren.

They made sure that several of the folks saw them enter Stanley's room. They held hands, and the touch was warm and comforting. Stanley went to the closet and put on the captain's jacket. Lauren chuckled. They sat upon the floor and opened the trunk. Stanley reached in, completed his sea wayfaring attire by putting on the captain's hat, and pulled out a piece of paper containing, coincidentally, another quote from Robert Browning:

> *The common problem, your's, mine, everyone's,*
> *Is — not to fancy what were fair in life*

Provided it could be, — but, finding first
What may be, then find how to make it fair
Up to our means: a very different thing!

Lauren thought this was a wonderful intellectual adventure. She reached into the trunk and pulled out the paper upon which the following appeared:

Love that hath us in the net,
Can he pass, and we forget?
Many suns arise and set;
Many a chance the years beget;
Love the gift is Love the debt.
          Even so
Love is hurt with jar and fret;
Love is made a vague regret;
Eyes with idle tears are wet;
Idle habit links us yet.
What is love? For we forget:
          Ah, no! no!

The Miller's Daughter
Alfred Lord Tennyson

Stanley put his arm around her sagging shoulders. She rested her head upon his chest. They were quiet. In the solitude, the game was no longer a game. The play had its private scene. They lay upon the bed and his arms enfolded her. He bent over and sealed their magical moment with a kiss. Young lips do have a certain sweetness. Old lips, even when parched and cracked, have a beguiling nectar. It is the taste of a confirmation of living, the unshakeable belief that only death can deprive the heart of its beat and the emotions it can engender. The splendor of love was revealed to have no bounds, no age. They entered a calm sleep. Dying bodies can share new life.

Later, after Lauren had returned to her room, Stanley just knew that Cindy would not have minded his finding some loving comfort in his closing days. In fact, she probably would have encouraged it. He sat at the desk and took the folded paper out of his wallet. It was a poem that Cindy had given him the day before she died. She had asked him to read it aloud. He had reread it many times after that. Elderly persons cry as youngsters do. It is spontaneous and the body throbs. He read the poem aloud now and then sobbed with a mixture of relentless memory and anticipation of a future, no matter how brief, of joined love. For an instant, he had a glimpse of forgotten dreams.

> *Remember me when I am gone away,*
> *Gone far away into the silent land;*
> *When you can no more hold me by the hand,*
> *Nor I half turn to go yet turning stay.*
> *Remember me when no more day by day*
> *You tell me of our future that you plann'd:*
> *Only remember me; you understand*
> *It will be late to counsel then or pray.*
> *Yet if you should forget me for a while*
> *And afterwards remember, do not grieve:*
> *For if the darkness and corruption leave*
> *A vestige of the thoughts that once I had,*
> *Better by far you should forget and smile*
> *Than that you should remember and be sad.*

> Remember
> Christina Georgina Rossetti
> (1830-1894)

FIVE

What is wrong with me?
What can the matter be?
It is a mystery!

She had couched it in terms of this short ditty that she recited over and over again to remind herself, or more accurately to confirm, that she was no longer the person she used to be. It is bad enough for an elderly person to sense the essence of life being drained from the body, and it adds frustration and despair to know that the mind once intact has now become tattered. It is a monumental task to hold it all together.

Violet Dubrow had been in the independent living wing for over three years. There had been many new arrivals, and many departures. The usual route was from independent living to assisted living and then unilateral death. The grave is the last resting home. Some, however, had escaped. She had befriended Georgia Haines, actually one of the few persons she had gotten friendly with. Georgia was miserable there. Her grandchildren were also unhappy that she was not in their midst. It was not Georgia's children that rescued her from this place, it was her heroic daughter-in-law, divorced from her son, who had the heart and gumption to take the older woman into her home. Violet would never forget the smiles of the grandchildren as they clung to Georgia when they came for her. Violet would never be that fortunate.

As a teenager, Violet had been one of the most popular girls in the high school of a small city not far from Philadelphia. She had been a pretty and vivacious girl, and she had many friends. People were drawn to her outgoing personality and good looks. She dated lots of boys, refusing to go steady with any of them. Her mother repeatedly advised her to play the field. That was the way to build up romantic memories to last a lifetime.

That outlook may have been a contributing factor to three failed marriages. The longest of the three had lasted just under two years. There had been no children, and if it were not for the hefty estate left to her by her parents she probably would have struggled financially. None of her husbands had been business or love achievers. Being economically comfortable in middle age she resigned herself to a life alone without men or sexual affection. She still had numerous friends, and she lost herself in social involvements such as concert and theater goings, card playing sessions, teas and other get-togethers. Nothing infringed on her outgoing mannerism and she spoke and acted her mind at will.

All of this changed gradually as her body and mind began to suffer from various ailments. Two operations left her morose and she gained excessive weight. Her early good looks transposed to gaunt expressions, and her confidence and assertiveness faded into a haunting withdrawal. Eventually, living alone was impossible, and her attorney found *Mountain Splendor* as a viable option. Here she was able to maintain a status quo. She did manage to develop some closeness with a few of the ladies but it was a strain and she was constantly nervous about sustaining such relationships. It was when Stanley arrived that her problem escalated.

It could have been any combination of factors that attracted her to him. She was entranced by his sense of humor and she felt an urge to cradle his frail body. He sure was a contrast to her rotund frame. She could not bring herself to say or do anything about this kind of feeling she thought she would never have again.

During one of the dance lesson sessions, she was placed next to him and the instructor told everyone to hold hands. His hand seemed small, but it thrilled her and she was tempted to give him a telltale squeeze. But, she could not bring herself to do that. She also tried to sit at the dining table he was at as often as she could without appearing obvious.

Now, a new woman had usurped any secret chance she might have of getting close to him. It surprised her that she could feel so jealous. It delighted her that she had such passion. In some ways it was sharper than she could recall these emotions as a youngster. If she could speak to anyone about it, she would describe it in theatrical terms. Each time she saw Stanley and Lauren together, holding hands or just talking, it was a dagger through her heart.

Jealousy has no age limitations, no chronological boundaries. Not that she would or could do anything about it. Yet, it depressed her knowing that she was so radically different from her former self. It made her think that the stigma of old age brought about self-imposed restrictions. It was as if the shackles of the body suppressed her will.

She hated to think she was reduced to the kind of person she never wanted to be, petty and vindictive. Yet, if Lauren were to be moved to the assisted living wing, Violet would try to muster up enough courage to make an overture to Stanley. That is, if she could overcome whatever limitations were affecting her free will. Lauren looked as if she were on her deathbed.

She was extremely pale and tentative in her motions. Certainly, she could not last much longer. The elderly are good at reading the signs of impending death. They have had much practice. They are in close proximity to those dire events on nearly a daily basis. Violet had never wished ill of anyone. She held no grudges against her former husbands even though they were instrumental in ushering forth her empty life. From her young years when she had such confidence and a positive image of herself, she did not like who she was now. Yet, that would not stop her from wishing for bad things. To be sour instead of happy in the waning days of life is truly a bitter pill to swallow.

She was not proud of herself when she complained to Carol about the disgusting open display of affection between Stanley and Lauren. The secret complaint was that she should have been in Lauren's place. Carol was very diplomatic in her response, particularly when Violet voiced the opinion that the two were disgracefully flaunting their relationship. It did not make Violet feel good when Carol told her that she was the only one who had complained so far. Carol said she would give it some thought, and was going to speak with Lauren's niece who was coming for a visit on Saturday. Violet, now a large lady, had become a little person.

SIX

Penny had received Carol's telephone message asking her to stop in to speak with her before she visited her aunt. There was no indication as to what it might be about, and Penny was just hoping that it was not about moving Lauren to assisted living because of her deteriorating health condition. Penny still felt badly about not keeping her aunt with her. If being in the home accelerated her aunt's decline, she would feel even worse.

Penny knocked at the office door. "Come in," Carol beckoned. The two ladies shook hands and Carol continued, "Nice to see you again."

"Good on my part as well."

They sat down together on the small sofa. Penny braced herself. "Well, I assume you have some news for me."

Carol started off hesitatingly. "I do not want to blow this out of proportion. So, let me just state the facts and then we can discuss the matter. Your aunt and a male resident have become fast friends, rather smitten I might add."

Penny grinned. "That's wonderful. I couldn't wish anything better for her in the limited time she has left."

"Normally, I would agree with you. But, for me, there is a larger picture. There have been complaints of such goings on. Your aunt and Stanley, and that is his name, have been making their signs of affection open and on going. It is almost as if they are purposely drawing attention to their behavior."

"I still think it is wonderful. The way I look at it, these two are consenting adults. It's nobody else's business."

"I wish it was as simple as that. We exist hear by word-of-mouth. Our reputation is our value. Any risk that it might become jaded, no matter how innocent or natural the events becomes a concern to our directors and that is passed down to me. It is my job to guard the high quality of this institution."

"I think a reputation is enhanced by the fact that there is a warm and friendly environment here."

"You and I may see it that way. Others, I am afraid, may object. Such can easily get out-of-hand. I do not want to lose my job for the appearance that there is no control among the residents."

"I still think it is making a mountain out of a mole hill. What do you want me to do? My aunt has more influence over me than I have over her."

"Maybe you can just suggest some discretion. Private affairs should remain that way. Hopefully, the uproar will die down."

"I can't guarantee anything. I'll see what she says. Thanks for the heads-up so I don't overtly show too much joy."

Lauren had just finished putting her books that were delivered the day before in the bookcase that Carol arranged for her. She had pulled out a couple of tombs to extract a quote to put in the treasure chest. She was enthralled by the concept of a treasure chest and was totally absorbed with Stanley in the pleasure of reaping the harvest of its contents. It did not take long to locate a first perfect candidate, and she printed it out on an index card that she had on the desk.

When all my griefs were shared with thee,
As all my hopes were thine —
As all thou wert was one with me,
May all thou art be mine!

Prefatory Poem to My
Brother's Sonnets
Alfred Lord Tennyson

Answering the knock on the door, she was greeted by a beaming Penny. They warmly embraced, and Lauren ushered her niece in and closed the door behind her.

"This is very nice," Penny offered as she looked around.

"It is a bit small, but it is clean and comfortable. The view is not as appealing here in the back as it is in the front. I find myself more in tune with nature these days."

"That's good. I don't ever recall you having an interest in the out-of-doors."

"You will learn that change is possible even in old age."

"No doubt. Carol asked me to stop in to see her before I came here. I thought it might be bad news. I am ecstatic that it is good news, really good news."

"So, she told you about Stanley?"

"Nothing about him in particular but just what you may have found together."

"Yes. That is the wonderful part. An old broad in love. The fullness I have now makes up for the emptiness of my early life. Of course, I didn't realize then what I was missing. And that is probably a good thing. The best that I can wish for you is that you find it for yourself now rather than later."

"Am I going to meet him?"

"Sure enough. He is right next-door. Tell me first what Carol wants from you."

"She is happy for you. She just suggested that some discretion might tone down any negative overtones. I guess she feels that suggestion might be more influential if it came from me."

"Another benefit of old age. There are no rewards in imposing artificial limitations or restrictions on behavior. I have never reaped the benefits of love before. I am sure not going to miss out on one second of it in my closing days just to placate a bunch of old biddies."

"Good for you. I am behind you all the way. I communicated what I was told, and that's the end of it for me. I am very happy for you, and you have my full encouragement to love to the utmost. I would welcome love in my life, but it just hasn't happened. I assure you I am totally receptive to it. It just seems like there are very few kind and gentle men out there. Does Stanley have an eligible son?"

"He has a son, but I sense this apple has fallen far from the tree."

"Too bad. Might have made for an interesting association."

"You are worthy of having a love in your life. It will come, I am sure. I hope I am still alive to see you as happy as I am."

"How are you feeling?"

"I'm sure no spring chicken, but love does diminish negative thoughts. I am probably no better than I was, but I feel renewed and alive. Love is a magic potion, and I am gulping it down straight from the bottle."

"You are funny in your old age. You have developed a sense of humor while here."

"Another credit in Stanley's column. Besides, no inhibitions prompt a diverse personality. The distance between humor and seriousness is easy to navigate over calm waters."

"A philosopher, as well."

"Just proves my point."

They went next door, and Penny met Stanley. He sure looked anemic and as frail a replica of her aunt as could be. Yet, his voice was rich and full, and there was no escaping the glitter in his eyes. Stanley was warm and easy going, and Penny chuckled to herself as the two oldsters in unison reached for each other's hand which they grasped the entire duration of the conversation. A symbolic lifeline is a saving gesture.

Penny accompanied them as their guest for lunch in the dining room, and then she headed home. She hugged the two elders, whispering in her aunt's ear, "I love him for loving you. Be happy."

For the entire drive home Penny had a warm glow in her heart. She could not wish more than this for her darling aunt, and it certainly made her decision not to keep her at home a fortuitous one. Carol just knew that her aunt's strong will matched by Stanley's and the two would prevail against all obstacles and outside forces. She wished her mother had found such happiness, and selfishly she clutched at a dream that her own life would be so enriched. It is the promise of tomorrow which nudges us gently forward.

SEVEN

Still basking in the glow of Penny's visit, it was that night that Lauren proposed they sleep together. Stanley readily agreed, and later in the night he slipped into Lauren's room.

Younger people are either ill informed or too prudish to think that elderly people can have and enjoy a sexual relationship. Actually, an act of love among older people can be very meaningful and most satisfying. Stamina and quick relief may be absent as with the younger set, yet a warm and enchanting closeness can be physically enjoyable and mind fulfilling for those that connect on a dimension that the young ignore. The pleasure can linger and endure.

After closing the door behind him, they embraced and kissed, a warm and tender kiss. Supporting each other's weak frame, breathing was labored. They sat upon the bed and Stanley read aloud a poem that he had pulled out of the treasure chest for this momentous occasion. Lauren clung to him. Here was the symbol of her love.

> *How thrills once more the lengthening*
> > *chain*
> > *Of memory, at the thought of thee!*
> *Old hopes which long in dust have lain,*
> *Old dreams, come thronging back again,*
> > *And boyhood lives again in me;*
> *I feel its glow upon my cheek,*
> > *Its fullness of the heart is mine,*
> *As when I leaned to hear thee speak,*
> > *Or raised my doubtful eye to thine.*

> *Yet hath thy spirit left on me*
> > *An impress Time has worn not out,*
> *And something of myself in thee,*
> *A shadow from the past, I see,*
> > *Lingering, even yet, thy way about;*
> *Not wholly can the heart unlearn*
> > *That lesson of its better hours,*

Not yet has Time's dull footstep worn
         To common dust that path of flowers.
Thus, while at times before our eyes
         The shadows melt, and fall apart,
And, smiling through them, round us lies
The warm light of our morning skies, —
         The Indian Summer of the heart!
In secret sympathies of mind,
         In founts of feelings which retain
Their pure, fresh flow, we yet may find
         Our early dreams not wholly in vain!

Memories
John Greenleaf Whittier

"With you," Stanley whispered in her ear, "I have glimpses of those early dreams. There can be no greater joy than to realize those dreams have not been totally forgotten."

"With you," Lauren responded in a soft whisper to match the peaceful tones of his remark, "I live new dreams every moment. Strange, I thought my life before you was satisfying, and it was in the sense that I felt a contentment inspiring and guiding young minds. Now, I know a life that is fulfillment for me. I am no longer a person alone, no longer an individual mind and heart. Togetherness can be so complete, so absorbing."

They knew they were both too physically restricted to reach any sexual climax, and even the chill of the night demanded that Stanley keep on his flannel pajamas and Lauren her wool sweat suit. That did not prevent them from holding each other closely, the warmth of bodily contact amidst gentle caresses and sweet kisses leading to a total comfort for body and mind. This too can be the ultimate act of love.

A peaceful sleep held them in that absorbing bond. The true measure of value for their remaining days had been recorded and stored.

They alternated sleeping in each other's room, messing up the unused bed so that the housekeeping staff would not guess of their private meetings. Since nobody else was up for their early trip to the dining room for breakfast, it was a relaxing venture all around.

The spring arrived warm and inviting, and unless it was raining they would walk ever so slowly to their love bench. No schedule impeded their wants and desires. There they would sit, talking at times, and mostly quiet with bodies touching as they sat. Hands were held and arms tenderly clutched. A world of their own that closed them in and shut others out. Love can be that powerful.

As the nights warmed, they shed their night attire and lay naked. That was as close as they could get physically. Brittle skin is no barrier to a thumping although aging heart. Yearning for that kind of closeness eases apprehension and softens any fleeting moments. The fruit of their mature love would not be denied. Lauren felt completely compensated for the loveless years. For Stanley, unimpeded by age and infirmity, his heart proved expansive and pliable. Cindy graciously moved aside to make room for Lauren.

The uproar over the aged lovers gradually dissipated. The elderly are in tune to accepting the inevitable. The beauty of the loving relationship became a natural part of the scene, and most came to admire the presence of a figment of youth in their midst.

Even Violet came around to view Lauren in a new light. She was no longer an adversary but an intimate friend. That turn of events occurred one afternoon when Stanley had been taken to the clinic in town for some tests that his far off doctors had ordered. All of the medical records of the residents were copied and housed at that clinic. There were physicians there who worked closely with the continuing care of other specialists. Lauren was hobbling down the hallway and stumbled. Violet had been coming from the other direction and instinctively reached out and was able to grab Lauren before she fell. She assisted her to a couch in the lounge. The two women talked openly for an hour. Violet's compassion, long dormant, emerged and easy conversation endeared the older and sicklier woman to her concern. They embarked on the road to friendship. Violet was pleased that this was an easier act than she thought, and over ensuing days a thread of intimacy developed between them.

Carol also had a new understanding and belief in what oldsters can find in one another. Stanley and Lauren dropped in often to chat with her, and these sessions were absorbing. The younger woman marveled at the mental clarity behind the clouded façade. The combined spirit was uplifting.

One day, when the two came to see her, the talk started out on a more serious front. As long as she had been there, and with dying a common event, any discussion about death still made her feel uncomfortable. Especially was this true with these two who under their circumstances were bursting with new life. Seeing her family members die brought home to Carol in vivid fashion the human vulnerability factor. Lauren and Stanley were housed in her heart and she was very concerned for and about them. Any inevitable moments she tried to dismiss preferring to concentrate on the present moments.

Stanley and Lauren sat in chairs before Carol's desk. Stanley had that usual beguiling glimmer in his eye, and it held Carol in rapt attention. "Here is the plan, young lady of our heart. Two major points for you to know about and to assure us that our wishes are met. We have talked this over extensively and are in total agreement. Since we do not know how much longer we have to be your guests here, if either one of us dies, or both of us, we want to be cremated and our ashes spread by the bench on the far side of the grounds. Lauren's niece has been informed of this as well. My son won't give a hoot just as long as nothing is required from him. If I die before Lauren, all of the possessions in my room are to be given to her. If she dies first, her things are to be given to me. Do we need to formalize this in any way?"

Carol could not halt the tears forming in her eyes. "I think it is enough that you have told me what you want. I will check with the attorney the home uses just to be sure. In the meantime I will prepare a letter that you can both sign and I can witness. This job carries with it many sad moments. Among the saddest will be to see either one of you pass on and the love you share come to an end. It is remarkable and is a lesson for us all."

Stanley smiled and patted the corner of the desk. "You are a special person in our life, just know that. Love does not end at death. Memories of that love are self-perpetuating in those special people we have touched and leave behind. John Greenleaf Whittier put it this way:

Proving in a world of bliss
What we fondly dream is this, —
Love is one with holiness!

We hope that the dream we are living is not forgotten. We know you are the kind of person that in your quiet moments you will have glimpses of what we have found together. It will bring anew an appreciation and a sustained life."

A tear rolled down Carol's cheek. Lauren nodded at her, a warm smile on the thin lips beneath the glasses was a love echo resounding in the small confines of the office.

They rose to leave. "One more thing," Stanley offered with as firm a voice as he could muster, "We would like to get married. Please let us know what licenses and blood tests are required. If it is at all possible, we would like to have the ceremony and reception here. This is our home and these are our friends."

"Most definitely. I am very happy for you both."

Lauren added, "We are happy for us, too."

EIGHT

Before the day was out, every person in the home knew about the wedding plan for Stanley and Lauren. At dinner, congratulatory expressions were numerous and lively. A new vitality was infused in the static hallways. For once, television viewing in the lounge took second place to the discussions about the pair tying the knot.

Even though Lauren had told her earlier, no one was more thrilled than Violet. Lauren had been instrumental in correcting her world and in redefining the outlook of her youth. She felt good about herself for the first time in a long dry period. How easily that can be transferred to feeling good for and about others. Violet was doubly pleased when Lauren asked her to help along with Carol and Penny to plan the reception. There would be no best lady, but if there had been one Lauren told her that Violet would have been the one she would have asked. Violet cringed recalling her earlier unsavory thoughts about Lauren. To be in the inner circle, she vowed to make it a memorable occasion for all.

As if the world was smiling on the forthcoming union, the following day was glorious. After breakfast, Stanley and Lauren walked slowly to their love bench. There they sat, hands clasped, sides touching. Birds serenaded them, flowers revealed their beauty and scent, and even the air had a freshness that could easily permeate old nostrils. Smells are not sharp for old folks, but there was no escaping that the aroma of the new day was special for them. It quivered with purity, and it kindled their personal glow. The sun was warm on their bodies and a gentle breeze carried inner thoughts to great heights. Surely it was a day for love, their day.

A restful silence merely bolstered the warm and tender feelings. Lauren was the first to speak in a gentle voice, so softly it did not disturb the silence but emphasized the quietness, "My dearest, did you know that a full heart can speak on its own?"

"Ah, and a full heart can be completely receptive."

"I cannot wish for any greater happiness than I have right now. I do wish we were in better health so that we can hold on to this happiness longer. I am content knowing that I have not been deprived of this kind of feeling, and I do pity those who never experience it."

He did not respond for a few minutes. "For us, a moment is an eternity. Young people waste precious time. We know how to grasp its total significance. A lifetime can be in a moment. Cindy and I had many years of love and happiness, certainly a lifetime. In this valuable brief period, another lifetime for me, we have the substance and totality of all dreams."

She leaned over and kissed his cheek. She placed her head on his shoulder. Her eyes were closed. She dozed off. His light kiss on her forehead preceded his helping her up and they started toward the home for lunch.

After lunch, they took a contented nap, holding tightly to each other and the moment. Carol then took them into town to take care of the pre-marriage requirements. Thomas had given his consent for his errant father to commit probably his last act of insanity. They met the Justice of the Peace, and he was amenable when he was told that the love couple would be writing their own vows for him to recite.

A long way off, Penny found it difficult to put her enthusiasm into the required visits to medical offices to offer samples and pitches for drug products. Her mind was on her aunt and the miraculous opportunity for her to have an exciting kind of happiness. That she might be a part of this kind of magic completely absorbed her. Every woman dreams of this kind of love. Better it should come in the winter of one's life than not at all. She might never find it. She would rather it be around the next bend in the road, or in the next week or month. Aunt Lauren's luck might rub off on her. Such a vivid hope supplies a spark of life.

Carol was also basking in the light-hearted mood of the place. This was a refreshing and uplifting event, and it bolstered her firm resolve to make the wedding special for Stanley and Lauren. That way it would be special for all, especially for her. There was a sincere closeness that she felt towards the loving couple, and this led to a fortification of her personal belief that old people can attain the happiness they so richly deserve. One might even say it is something they earned by plodding through a life that is often filled with stumbling blocks and harsh realities. They should never be shortchanged. The price of living is already too high. Carol knew it would be better if she were more detached from the situation and that her personal well being hung on the edge of a cliff by getting so close to the two people. She could not help it. They had endeared themselves to her, and she loved them dearly.

Carol called Penny with an idea. This wedding and its effect on the home and its residents would make a revealing and heart-warming magazine article or television documentary. Penny liked the idea, although she suspected that her aunt and Stanley wanted to keep it all as private as possible. Carol would approach them with the idea, and if they agreed to it then Penny would attempt to make some contacts with the media.

Carol stopped by to see them just before dinner. When she entered the room at their invitation, she was enamored to see them sitting on the floor going through the papers in the trunk. It was a glorious sight, almost like two children playing together. Stanley had on a sea captain's hat and lifted it slightly off of his head in the greeting. Both thought it was a good idea to take the wedding public, not so much for them but as a needed revelation of the feelings, desires and sensitivity of older Americans. Just because one is old and even infirm does not mean that there can be no goals and no fresh beginnings.

A major network picked up on the idea right away. An array of production personnel and equipment would descend upon the home the day before the wedding to set up and get some preliminary interviews and footage. The Board of Directors of the home was quite pleased with the developments and the possibility of good publicity for the institution. Carol was complemented for her initiative. At times, a natural action just happens to be the right thing to do.

Stanley and Lauren made the composition of the vows an exciting and memorable time. They drafted variations all of the time knowing that the final version would be straight forward from their hearts. The words might not fully capture that but they would try to get as close to it as possible. Carol gave them a sheet of paper with a rainbow in the upper right-hand corner for the completed document.

> *On this day, a beautiful day by any inner standard,*
> *Stanley and Lauren are joined in marriage. This*
> *ceremony is the public acknowledgement of hearts*
> *and minds already intertwined. As they enjoy the*
> *fruits of their love, they wish everyone to partake*
> *in its magnificence. It symbolizes more than just the*
> *cohesion of two individuals. It represents the*
> *glorious discovery of love that can occur at any*
> *age. It is the public recognition that old people have*
> *no less feeling, no less emotion, no less passion than*
> *younger people. It is an act of social defiance. The*
> *elderly do not just take up time and space with worthless*
> *thoughts and complaints. They can and will explore*
> *every facet of living and revel in the adventure. Until*
> *their last breath, old people cannot and will not be denied.*

By clasping hands, Stanley and Lauren signify the loving union of hearts and minds. Now as husband and wife, they are one. Let this serve as a model for all who are receptive to love at any age.

NINE

There is really no good moment to be put into a nursing home. Yet, if one has to enter the confines of such a place, a fortuitous opportunity would be at such a one as *Mountain Splendor* while it was in the throes of the forthcoming marriage. The spirits of the inhabitants were totally uplifted and the atmosphere was nearly festive. Surely, every bright light in the building was aglow reflecting hearts assured that dreams can be lived.

Such was the good fortune of Henry Hubbell. There had been scant good fortune in his life and before this it would not have been his definition of a bountiful occurrence to be forced into a place like this.

Mountain Splendor accepted a minimum number of charity cases. The department of Social Services had run out of options for the elderly and ailing Mr. Hubbell. A room in the independent wing was available, and the social worker assigned to the case assured Carol that the cantankerous man was still able to take care of himself but could not sustain himself at the rural trailer he had lived in before his heart attack.

Henry had always lived on the poverty borderline. His trailer was just some thirty miles away from the home. Never having a family and never married, he had lived in the run-down trailer in which his uncle raised him. As the only heir, he inherited the trailer and small mountain tract on which it was located right along a main road when the uncle passed away. There was no electricity and no plumbing. Henry spent countless hours gathering wood for the small wood stove he used for heating and cooking. The uncle's decrepit truck finally gave way and Henry had to walk the three miles to town to get supplies which he pulled back on a small carriage.

He had not finished high school, and gradually he turned into what most would refer to as a typical mountain man. His unruly hair grew long and the course beard nearly obliterated an oval face. He was small in stature but due to the exertion of hard physical labor he was muscular.

When he was a teenager, he had found an old clock in a dumpster. Evidently, someone had become frustrated and disenchanted with it and abandoned it. Henry took it back to the trailer, studied it and by tinkering with it got it running. He discovered the workings were much simpler than he would have imagined. After he had it running for a while, he sold it to an antique shop in the town. The shop gave him a couple of other clocks for him to work on, and gradually he gained a reputation as a clock repairman.

Other shops in the area started using him, and people would also bring him clocks to fix. A small shed behind the trailer was loaded with all sorts of items that his uncle had gathered over the years and Henry became adept at making clock parts if any were needed. He was able to eke out a bare living as the years passed. The older he got, the more erratic he looked and behaved, and eventually people stopped bring clocks to him as they were wary of him. He had overheard one person describe him as a man who had fallen off the turnip wagon.

At age seventy-one he had the massive heart attack. Since the trailer was off a main road, a passerby telephoned the sheriff's office describing what she thought was a body in the yard. How long he had been there that way nobody knows but the hospital doctor thought it was miraculous he was still alive when the ambulance brought him in. He was revived, but the prognosis was not encouraging. Social welfare was contacted when he could not pay the hospital and he was declared in no condition to return to the trailer. The heart attack left him extremely weak and with visual body tremors.

The State took over the property and condemned it. Henry retrieved two favorite clocks and a small duffle bag of clothes. These were the belongings that he brought with him when the social worker dropped him off at the home.

Henry had thought he had died for sure and had gone to heaven. Having a clean and comfortable room with electric lamps, a bathroom, and three satisfying meals a day, he figured he should have discovered a way of getting here sooner.

Carol introduced him to the crowd at one of the meals, and the folks got a charge out of seeing his ratty attire and hearing him speak with a guttural drawl. It was Stanley and Lauren who overtly welcomed him, and then he was accepted. Violet, with her newfound flair for life, found Henry refreshingly different from any of the other male residents and any of her former husbands. She might even have some romantic designs on the new arrival. Of course, she had no way of knowing that Henry had a fear, unwarranted as it might be, of fat people.

Carol let Henry set up his two clocks in the lounge as long as he promised to keep them wound. There were complaints that the chiming interfered with listening to the television, so he had to relocate them to the dining room. There they occupied a prominent place on a shelf above the sideboard, and he kept a watchful eye on them. They had always been a soothing presence in his life, and they had been faithful and trouble-free companions. Clocks have been around for centuries, and the word "clock" is derived from the Latin "clocca." He often wished they could speak because they would probably have some interesting stories to tell. Over the span of many years they had probably been in a number of households and had seen much of history unfold. They represented items that could still work even though well over one hundred years old. What other consumer product could brag that way? His own ticker might just keep on going that long as well.

TEN

It was the third night before the wedding. They were to sleep in Stanley's room that night. After dinner, they relaxed for a while and decided to go to sleep early, as they were tired.

Lauren emerged from the bathroom prepared to shed her clothing to sleep as close to him as physically possible. She had never been naked with a man at any early period of her life and would have been shocked if it had come to pass. One cannot associate nakedness with desire unless it is accompanied by a loving sensation. With Stanley, it just seemed the natural order of their love. Skin molded to skin is soul soldered to soul.

Stanley was lying on his side turned away from her and curled up. He was still dressed and laying on top of the bed cover. He turned his head towards her, and said in a voice weaker than she had heard before, "Please hold me."

Lauren swallowed and moved as swiftly as she could and lay behind him. She put her arm around him and hugged dearly. His voice was weaker yet and trailed off, "I love you.............I'm sorry."

The tears swelled up in her aging eyes, blurring her glasses, and the tears streamed down her face. She would not release her hold on him even as soreness seeped into her limbs. She stroked his face, the flesh already turning cold. As if a child again, she cried herself to sleep. She awoke as the first light of the dawning streaked across the sky. She whispered in an ear that could no longer hear but to a still heart which she believed would know what she was saying. "I will always love you, always and forever."

Lauren got off the bed and went to the telephone. She dialed Carol's internal number.

Carol was half awake when the telephone rang. It brought her to full attention. There is something menacing about a phone call at odd hours. "Hello."

"This is Lauren. Stanley is.........gone."

The siren of the ambulance is an especially ominous sound for nursing home residents. It is the calamitous announcement of a health condition drastically changed for the worse or of a life terminated. By mid-morning all knew that Stanley had died. The reverie came to a screeching halt and a pall descended over the place.

Violet stayed by Lauren's side in her room as she rested upon the bed. She felt Lauren's pain, and her compassion swelled to almost a bursting point.

After doing what she had to do, Carol locked herself in her office. She telephoned Penny with the sad news and then put her face down on her arms on the desk and sobbed uncontrollably.

Since his uncle's death long ago, Henry had not been close to anyone dying. He could understand his own death since he had been brought so close to it. It was nothing he could explain, and he was not sure what it all meant. He was not even sure what to do. The only thing that crossed his mind was a symbolic act that turned out to be expressive for so many. He stopped the pendulums and covered the clocks.

Penny arrived the next day and comforted her aunt as best as she could. Lauren had a far off look in her eyes, and she only muttered a few words. She would not leave her room and she would not eat. The turn of events had hastened her downward spiral. Penny stayed in the room overnight, sleeping fitfully in the chair.

The next day, Stanley's ashes were delivered. They had to put Lauren in a wheelchair, and Carol, Penny and Violet took her to the bench. The sky was cloudy and a hint of rain hovered above the mountains. Carol scattered the ashes around the bench and the four women cried and held hands.

Lauren was moved to an assisted living room. Violet insisted on bringing her the meals, although Lauren barely touched any of them. Now bed-ridden, life seeped out of the sickly body. Penny, Carol and Violet were by her bed as she took her last breath. Lauren said nothing but did reach for Penny's hand with the last strength her body could muster. The three women hugged and tears once again fell from swollen eyes.

Mountain Splendor was quiet and only the basic activities were undertaken. Nobody talked about it but the air was heavy with grief. Many of the residents stayed in their rooms, perhaps contemplating the inevitable end facing us all. The clocks, now lifeless, remained covered.

ELEVEN

The following few days were very trying for Carol, her staff and the residents of the home. The deaths of Stanley and Lauren were hard enough to bear since they had symbolized the potential vitality of the institution. Then, at dinner, Henry had another serious heart attack and died instantly, collapsing heavily right on the table laden with dishes and food. It shocked the others at the table and the dire event reverberated throughout the dining room. Meals were left unfinished as all rushed out to the sanctity of their rooms. Fear of the inevitable can lead to quiet but restless contemplation.

Carol was extremely proud of her staff. All were local recruits, and they were caring and diligent country folk. Carol held extensive interviews before hiring anyone, and she would not bring anybody on board who did not advocate and display a caring attitude towards people. Too many horror stories about nursing homes abounded, such as aides falsifying records of feedings and bathing when in fact little or none were done and even downright physical and mental abuse of residents. None of that would be tolerated here. Yet, even three deaths in a brief span of time can deflate the motivation and spirit of the best intended.

Stanley and Lauren's rooms had been cleaned out and all of their possessions were put in Carol's office. Henry's clocks, still covered, were moved there as well. As she stared at the vestiges of people's lives, primarily the trunk that housed heaps of hand-written quotations and printed pages from various sources, she wondered how or who would bolster her morale.

Since Stanley died first, as agreed everything was Lauren's. Penny was due to come on the weekend to spread Lauren's ashes and select whatever she might want from the personal effects. If she did not want the stack of books, Carol thought she might try to expand the meager home library although the books were too erudite for most of the residents and not light reading. There would also be the problem of who might care for them since the staff was already stretched thin and employment funds were being cut in the poor economy.

The network had cancelled the project when informed of Stanley's death. The reasoning was fuzzy but apparently it was thought the program would be too depressing.

Carol held a staff meeting at which she tried to infuse a revived spirit to the crowd. The staff and the residents had been looking forward not only to the wedding but also the television taping of it and the background. Carol carefully explained that they all needed to view death as fortifying the meaning of life and to not let it negate their efforts. Rather, it should be regarded as an addition to the display of courage to care for those who still needed their help so badly. She sensed the message was being conveyed. By rallying the others, it did uplift her spirits and resolve slightly. However, it did not stop her crying when she returned to her office and saw those left behind possessions of vital lives. Stanley had called it glimpses of forgotten dreams. What were her dreams? The yesterdays were spoken for. Could there be dreams for tomorrow? Would there be any chance of them ever being realized? What would tomorrow bring?

In the quiet of the evening, Penny was lost in the thoughts of her aunt. It brought back the memories of her mother and the inviting family times that they had all spent together. One particular Christmas was vivid in her mind. She was seven, and Aunt Lauren had given her a beautiful musical trinket box. On the lid was a painting of a little girl hugging a puppy, and the music it played when the lid was lifted was Lara's Theme from Dr. Zhivago. That box was on her desk, where it had always been with her. She sat down at the desk and opened the lid listening intently to the melodic tune. In the box was a space for small objects. All of the quarters she had received from the tooth fairy were there. The tears again flowed freely. Aunt Lauren had found real love so late in life. Why couldn't she have been able to enjoy it just a little bit longer?

Penny's thoughts quickly shifted to her disillusionment with the network for canceling the taping of the documentary. After all, the beautiful love story was still there even if the participants were no longer around, and the message of old timers having feelings and being complete people too was perhaps even more powerful under the circumstances. Also, the story of a caring and involved nursing home needed to be told to offset the bad ones out there. It would give society an inside look at a story and place that should be aired. It might give some elderly people without family to take care of them something to attach to and not to dread the option. Remaining days can be spent in a friendly and warm environment to ease travel through the final days.

It took her less than an hour to compose the letter on her computer. She mailed it to the President of the network the next day by certified mail. At least she was doing something. The nagging thought took a firm hold; more, much more needs to be done.

When Penny entered Carol's office, the two women hugged. They were silent for a moment, an interlude to once again let the significance of recent developments fully settle in.

Carol spoke first, her voice raspy. "Stanley left everything to Lauren. His son told me to do with everything as I wish. Sadly, he did not even comment on his father's passing. There are things in this world I do not understand and probably never will. It is puzzling how a sensitive and deep person can wind up with a hard and cold child. Well, anyway, everything is over there in the corner. There are books and some personal items, a few antiques, including that lovely trunk chock full of beautiful sayings that Stanley and his wife accumulated over a lifetime. Lauren was enchanted by it all, and the two of them dug into it as children looking for buried treasure. It grew to mean much to her."

Penny went over to the trunk, opened it, and could just see why this would have been a part of her aunt. "I'd like to keep the trunk. It will be a reminder of a beautiful life, no two beautiful lives."

"I am glad. I would, if you don't mind, like to keep the captain's hat that he wore when he delved into the trunk. It rounds out a heroic image I have of him. I think I will keep the other antique items, just as you feel, as a memento of a special love. I thought I would put the books in our library, but it won't be feasible. I'll give them to the public library in town if they want them. Do you want to look through them and keep any of them?"

"Sure. Please do keep the hat. It will have far more meaning for you than for me."

The two women looked at all of the books. Penny selected a few that she remembered seeing prominently on her aunt's shelves. Carol picked out a few that had beautiful leather bindings.

"I wrote to the President of the network," Penny spoke slowly, "asking that they reconsider taping the documentary. I firmly believe it would be beneficial all around."

"Good for you. The story should be told."

"If the network doesn't do it, maybe we can figure some other way to do it."

"Yes, by all means. Let's do that."

The two women went by Violet's room, and the three women went out to the bench to scatter Lauren's ashes to be with Stanley. It was another moment to shed tears, to hug, and to reaffirm that the memory of these two special people would stay in their hearts.

TWELVE

The next morning Violet went to Carol's office. "Do you have a minute?"

"Yes."

Violet sat down before the desk. "I am feeling real guilty about my early visit to you complaining about Stanley and Lauren. Getting close to them showed me not only how wrong I was but also how very mean spirited I had been. Being with Lauren, becoming her friend, taught me that I can be a beautiful person as they were. I hope I never have another evil thought."

Carol smiled. "That would be nice, wouldn't it? After all is said and done, and at the end of the day, we are all only human. We have faults and weaknesses. The secret is to come back stronger once you have realized that. I think you have learned that well."

"Having remorse may not enough. I feel I need to do something constructive to celebrate their memory. Can you think of anything I can do?"

Carol thought for a moment. "One thing does come to mind. Those books stacked in the corner were their personal books. I thought about putting them in our library here, but I have no one to do that or to look after them. The alternative is to give them to the town library. Would you be willing to set them up in our library and keep your eye on them?"

Violet smiled broadly. "You have found your librarian."

Within the hour, Violet returned with a cart and in two trips she had taken all of the books to the library room and had arranged them on a vacant shelf in alphabetical order. She then carefully made a hand-written sign that she placed above the books:

THESE ARE THE PERSONAL BOOKS OF
STANLEY VERITAN AND LAUREN
CHASTNER. THEY ARE PLACED HERE
IN HONOR OF THEIR LOVING AND
LASTING MEMORY.

TOUCH THEM, READ THEM, AND
TAKE THEM TO YOUR HEART.
PLEASE HANDLE WITH CARE.

A week later Penny received a reply letter from the President of the network. The tone was cordial but unsympathetic. It explained that the decision not to tape the documentary was duly reconsidered and it would not be reversed. Because of a gloomy national economic outlook, the network felt that its public service functions would be better met by offering programming that might uplift spirits rather than by portraying deaths causing the cancellation of a planned happy event. Of course, the network missed the point entirely. Penny could only blame herself. Perhaps her letter was not clear or forceful enough.

A few days later, it dawned on her how to get the network to change its decision. It needed to be pressured. The network had to be inundated by letters, e-mail messages and telephone calls. Penny called Carol and asked her to check Stanley's file for the name of the school he taught at. Lauren had told her about the throng that came from all over the nation to the retirement celebration for Stanley and Cindy. When Penny called the school, they readily agreed to send the list they had used to contact the former students, and there was even an asterisk placed by each that had attended the event.

Penny gasped with amazement when she received the list. It could easily have been a recital of the rich and famous. Corporate directors, large business owners, politicians, Hollywood celebrities, sports figures, and people throughout the arts were on the list. Among the politicians were three members of the House of Representatives of the Congress of the United States. Penny would use most of the money she had put aside to give to *Mountain Splendor* for any extra needed care for Aunt Lauren to formulate and expedite a mail campaign to each person on the list. The story was heart-warming and the reasons compelling for going forward. Contacting the network was suggested. She was sure this was the right tact. That was validated by the overwhelming response. Not only did the network buckle under the weight of the saturated contacts, many sent money to Penny for ongoing efforts.

Penny met with her lawyer friend who advised and formed for her a not-for-profit corporation for the purposes of advocating, establishing and urging the strict enforcement of the highest possible standards of health, safety and well being of nursing home residents. The organization was appropriately named LAURSTAN.

The taping took two days although the result would be a thirty-minute spot. After a panoramic view of *Mountain Splendor*, the camera focused in on Carol sitting at her desk. She introduced herself, and she explained about the home, the residents, staff, and the various activities such as art and sculpting classes, dance lessons, and instructive lectures. The camera caught snapshots of each of these activities in turn. Then, Penny was introduced and she narrated the love story of Stanley and Lauren. She described their mutual teaching backgrounds, the shared respectful admiration of the great poets and the masters of literature, and their similar frail physical condition. The camera focused on the library shelf of books and Violet's sign. It then moved along the grounds to the bench the lovers walked to and where their ashes were spread. Carol then closed the taping with the expressed disappointment of unfulfilled wedding plans, but with the moral that the two were every bit in love as two could be, that even after death their essence and what they had lived on in the spirit of the home, and that old people are whole, valuable and deserve to be helped and respected. The closing days for our elder citizens should be in a warm, peaceful and caring nursing home environment if families are unavailable or unable to provide this. The segment was powerful stuff. When it was aired, public opinion was extremely positive and the show called a high success.

Carol and Penny had decided not to mention the antique trunk, as it was so personal to the loving pair. Yet, it had a growing profound effect on Penny. In her quiet moments, she too was drawn to the treasure chest to find solace in a poem, story or saying. That evening, she pulled out a poem by Alfred Lord Tennyson.

> *Sweet, they tell me that the world is*
> *hard, and harsh of mind,*
> *But can it be so hard, so harsh, as those*
> *that should be kind?*
> *That matters not. Let come what will; at*
> *last the end is sure,*
> *And every heart that loves with truth is*
> *equal to endure.*

The Flight

In the quiet of that same night, Carol walked outside and gazed up at the stars. She whispered into space, "Yes, Stanley, dreams are not forgotten for the people who are remembered with love."

THIRTEEN

To Penny's utter surprise and pure delight, contributions kept pouring in for LAURSTAN. Many were accompanied by sad stories of relatives suffering through their last days in nursing homes. It reached a point where she had to quit her job and devote full attention to the purposes of the organization. She never would have guessed that she would have wound up to be an activist in a cause that had become near and dear to her heart. Now that she was fully immersed in it, it just seemed as if it was meant to be. Her mother and Aunt Lauren would surely have been proud of her.

It got so out-of-hand that she had to lease office space and hire two people to run it while she made trips to the nursing homes throughout the northeast where she would tour the facility, show the tape to the staff and residents, and attempt to hold out *Mountain Splendor* as a model institution. She would interview residents and staff in an attempt to formulate needed improvements and field suggestions for innovations. The next step was to register as a lobbyist and to pressure State legislators to enact fully protective legislation for State institutions. The Members of Congress who were Stanley's pupils promised to draft and introduce additional expansive federal legislation that would cover private institutions where occupants were admitted from other States and authority for such enactments would thereby fall within the foreign commerce provision of the Constitution.

Penny had never been in the position to hire people to work for her, and it was not an easy task. A number of good people applied. She thought it best if she found an additional connection so that a person working there have personal experience with the aged, particularly at a retirement or nursing home.

The story of Lacey Yazlow was heartbreaking on its own. Her parents divorced when she was eight, her mother leaving to be with another man. The mother had found her professor husband dull and incapable of making sufficient money to fuel a lifestyle she coveted. So, when a dashing playboy came along, she sunk her tentacles into him and off they went. Lacey's father, a history professor at Boston Community College, lost his job teaching there as the result of a reduction in force and was compelled to take on a menial labor job to support himself and Lacey. They barely made ends meet living in a one-bedroom apartment, and Lacey had the bedroom while her father slept on the sofa in the living room. They managed, and even were able to find some happy times together as Lacey grew older and they became quite close.

When Lacey was twelve, her father's mother had a series of strokes. She had been living alone and struggling in her own way. Lacey was very fond of her grandmother, a spirited elder who made Lacey laugh repeatedly. She needed all the laughs she could get. There was no choice but to have her placed in a State nursing institution. Lacey and her father visited her several times a week but she gradually grew weaker and no longer recognized them. She slipped away apparently in great pain, and the resident doctor would not give her anything to ease the way even with an angry outburst by her father. Only later did they come to realize that the grandmother's care had been substandard and uncaring. Her grandmother's plight and suffering left a lasting impression on Lacey. She swore to herself that she would become a nurse and care for the elderly as a tribute to her grandmother. Now eighteen, she was looking for employment to pay for the evening nursing school classes in which she was enrolled. This job at LAURSTAN was tailored made for her. She could devote time and energy to help in some ways for doing good for the aged. Penny's impression fortified that premise of the young woman's character. Lacey's father had recently been hired back at the college and slowly they were getting their lives in some semblance of order.

The other hiree was an older woman, some thirty years older than Lacey. Helen Finch had worked at several nursing homes as an aide and at each one had become disenchanted with the shoddy way they were run and the obstacles imposed on her that constantly frustrated her in the care of the residents. She simply wanted to help, but rules and regulations tied her hands and endless paperwork took a large chunk of her time. When she saw the advertisement for this job at LAURSTAN, it was obvious to her that she might do more good this way. She had talked it over with the man she had been living with but never married, and he encouraged her to apply. He knew better than to stand in the way of this principled and determined woman. When Penny brought her on board, Helen quit the current nursing home job she had.

It did not take long for Penny to be totally dependent and trustful of these two ladies in her absence. She even solicited their opinions and feedback, and was uplifted in knowing that they were eager, dedicated and creative in any new directions the organization might turn. Helen seemed to be a composite of her mother and Aunt Lauren, and Penny admired her greatly. Lacey was looked upon as a daughter. With the addition of such able assistance, Penny felt extra good about what she was doing.

The only thing lacking at this point was that she truly wanted Carol to be here with her. Carol's dedication, qualifications and professionalism would complete the areas where Penny was lacking. Penny's enthusiasm and stern resolve were her strong points. Between the two of them they could cover the national nursing home arena and not be limited geographically. Yet, she knew how Carol felt about her job at *Mountain Splendor* and the people there. It would take an unusual inducement for Carol to abandon that family.

FOURTEEN

Carol was fielding her own busy time. Since the broadcast of the documentary, not only had there been a surge in applications to *Mountain Splendor* but officials and nursing home administrators from around the nation were clamoring for a visit and a tour of the facility.

Carol had left Stanley and Lauren's rooms vacant as long as possible, not just as a tribute to them but also to salve her own emotional despair of losing them. Eventually, however, she had to place two newcomers in the rooms. A connection with those she had lost had come from a unique source. She was fond of Henry's clocks, and had mastered winding them and keeping them running. She placed them prominently on a table by her desk along with Stanley's sea captain's hat, and she would stare at them from time-to-time and warm memories would cascade into her being. Warm memories are the most endearing and enduring. The ticking and chiming of the clocks were also soothing and reassuring. The clocks were alive and marking gifted moments. The captain's hat was a symbol of boundless imagination, a confirmation and reassurance that all things dreamed are possible of achievement.

Tucker Atwood, by any objective or subjective standard, had lived an interesting and varied life. He had been a rock and roll singer in the 1950s, an off-Broadway actor, and a writer for television. He had never married, although he had come close several times. Caught in rituals of a life in which he had total control, he just did not see the advantage of trying to adapt to another person. He had no desire for children, due in part to his own loveless and aloof upbringing. Loneliness only set in when his usefulness became paramount. At age seventy, the television industry let him go and the union failed to back his cause. There just did not seem anything worthwhile to do. Anything he tried he quickly became bored with. He knew age was taking its toll not just because his memory started to fade but he lost patience easily and became frustrated quickly. This was followed by failure of his body to follow his mental instructions, and at the age of eighty-one he was about to enter *Mountain Splendor*. It was more than a let down. It was an utter failure of an active life and a creative talent. It had all of the attributes of death except he was still breathing.

Carol could tell right away that Tucker had a chip on his shoulder, and the last thing she needed was a new resident with an attitude problem.

When she showed him to his room, Lauren's room, all he did was grunt. She was tempted to offer him a lecture on fitting in and decided to hold off for a few days to see if he warmed up to the surroundings. At his first meal, she would seat him next to Violet and her newfound positive outlook might just rub off on him.

As it turned out, Violet's light-hearted mannerism failed to evoke any extended or friendly conversation. Tucker was not about to open up to a stranger, particularly one who talked incessantly. He did enjoy the food, and he would gulp down the company. Making the best of a bad situation was not new to him, but there was no way that he was going to enjoy it.

It was Dora Kinfelder's eighty-fourth birthday, and the way she was celebrating it was by entering a nursing home. She had been living in the town just across the line in Maine. Her older sister's house had been a refuge for her after her husband of more than fifty years had died. Her sister, Matty, had also been a widow and it was her marital home. Matty's two grown children were in California and time and distance can cause blood relations to run cold. Matty died two years ago, and Dora's growing fragility forced her to abandon the house and move to *Mountain Splendor*. She probably would have been forced to move somewhere anyhow as Matty's children inherited the house and were anxious to get proceeds from its sale. The early permission they extended to Dora to stay on was wavering.

Dora and Matty had always been close, even as children. They had shared secrets as well as boyfriends. Dora loved children but her husband was impotent, so she tried to enjoy Matty's children although she then lived halfway across the nation. Dora had a career as a journalist, and eventually she wrote a syndicated column that appeared weekly in nearly every major newspaper as well as a slew of smaller local newspapers. She had a knack for personalizing current events so that readers gained a greater understanding of what was going on. That was years ago, a lifetime away. She doubted that many would even recognize her name now. Life is full measure while one is useful. Once that usefulness is diminished, the vial of life's elixir has been emptied out.

So, here she was with no one to celebrate her birthday with and a body rebelling against independence. She was being put on a shelf, and a nondescript label would be all that she had to show for it. The clean and comfortable room, Stanley's old room, made no impression on her. It was merely a place to park her decrepit body as the grave beckoned. The expression she had used in her column at opportune moments, taken from writings of James Russell Lowell, *milestones into headstones*, seemed most appropriate now.

Carol was having more ideas lately than she knew what to do with. She called Penny. "I have an idea for you,"

"Why am I not surprised?" Penny's response was accompanied by a guttural chuckle.

"I think I have caught Stanley's overactive mind. It never fails to amaze me how we pick up on the patterns of others."

"In this case for the good."

"Well, here goes an idea for your consideration. Two new residents came in today. As far as I can tell they are both disenchanted with becoming old age waste products. A definite contrast to Lauren and Stanley. I couldn't keep those rooms empty any longer and I have put them in there. Maybe the remnants of love and tolerance will seep into their bones. Anyway, according to their files they both have extensive writing backgrounds. Tucker Atwood wrote for television, and Dora Kinfelder had a national newspaper column for many years. Perhaps, you can use their talent and I can get them involved in something to turn the head of the wild beast."

"Carol, you have had another stroke of genius. I wish I had you by my side so we might conquer the world together."

"That would probably be nice, but I am having difficulty just keeping this little world together."

"I can hope, can't I?"

"Always. Anyway, why don't you come up and meet them. Any proposal would have more credence coming from you."

"Actually, I have been thinking of a periodic newsletter, to be sent by e-mail and snail mail, keeping contributors and others abreast of developments and educating them on the rights and conditions we are fighting for. Unfortunately, my schedule is all jammed up. How about I send Lacey? Her youth and vitality are great selling virtues and might just be contagious. I would love for you to meet her and you two get to know each other."

"Fine. Just let me know when and she can have lunch with me."

Before Lacey's visit, Tucker and Dora did meet. As same-day arrivals, Carol introduced them both at dinner to the residents, and as next-door neighbors they passed a few times in the hallway. There were cordial salutations but no conversation. There was no reason to speak at length.

Carol and Lacey hit it off immediately, just as Penny knew they would. Carol had a natural way with people, and speaking to the youngster was easy and refreshing. Lacey was effervescent and idealistic, qualities Carol admired.   Lacey wanted to address her as Miss Seton but Carol insisted the youngster use her first name. Lacey talked extensively about her life, including her professor father, as well as her nursing studies and all of the projects she was working on at LAURSTAN. She also raved about Penny not only as a boss but also as a decent and dedicated person.

At lunch, Carol went around and asked Tucker and Dora to stay for a few minutes after the meal. They agreed to do that.

Both of the new arrivals had heard the stories about Stanley and Lauren and the video leading to the creation of LAURSTAN. After all, both were topics of close and keen interest among the residents. Lacey jumped ahead in her youthful way to tell them that the organization wanted to put out a newsletter, quarterly to start with, detailing the work of the staff and to present information on and about conditions in nursing homes and the rights of the elderly. She proposed that they collaborate and write these newsletters jointly.

Tucker and Dora looked at each other and then at Carol. Dora was the first to speak. "Writing is still second nature to me, maybe even a passion. Sure, I would love to write this newsletter, but I am not sure I know enough either about what you are doing or that much about senior rights. I probably should be ashamed to admit this."

"My sentiments exactly," Tucker chimed in.

Lacey, as bubbly as ever, responded, "I will keep you posted on everything you need to write about concerning LAURSTAN."

"And I," Carol interjected, "have an extensive personal library in my office for you to bone up on the subject matter."

Both oldsters smiled, and Carol knew it was going to be rewarding. "We'll do it," they said nearly in unison.

FIFTEEN

Since there were only the two of them, they usually ate at the table in the kitchen. Sitting across from Lacey at the small table, Owen Yazlow listened intently as his daughter gushed forth with the story of meeting Carol and then Tucker and Dora. Lacey barely had touched the food on her plate she was so excited about her experience and the prospects. It was not daunted in the second telling of the entire scenario as she had poured it all out to Penny and Helen earlier at the office. Lacey was particularly drawn to Carol and spoke of her in glowing terms.

Owen was extremely proud of his daughter. They had been through some major upheavals in the years since his wife left them. The hardships and then the sorrow of losing her grandmother had steadfastly matured the young woman. She was levelheaded and yet steeped with high aspirations. For all they had been through, Lacey still had a belief in the goodness of people and had the will to help whenever she could. This was a far cry from his own hapless youthful exploits where little had any meaning and he was unable to believe that life held any promise for him. Then came his big mistake by deceivingly becoming infatuated with the first woman who directed attention to him. Each saw what was not really there, and a disappointing reality brought personal tragedy. Lacey was the only good that had emerged from it.

That was then. Now, upon being rehired at the college, he had gained a firm hold of his bearing and was setting a true course. His outlook was positive and he found new enjoyment in teaching as well as in the various aspects of history that he had always been fascinated by. He had become a better teacher and a more responsive father. The college had even recently given him greater credence and authority. Without his mind being cluttered by extraneous remorse and guilt feelings, he was able to fully enjoy Lacey's telling of the events.

With all of this came the realization that he was aging without the closeness of female companionship. Finally accumulating some savings, he was hoping he and Lacey might find a house and he could get her the dog she had always wanted. There would be an opportunity for other things, including a wife if he could find a woman who could be a part of his changed and calmer disposition. Looking at the world with revitalized eyes, due in large part to his caring daughter who would probably not be with him forever, middle age can be imbued with a youthful spirit. There may not be total control over physical deterioration, but age can also be a state of mind. Lacey had confirmed that by the meeting with Tucker and Dora. Lacey had guessed when they eventually smiled it took years off their bearing. They had probably not smiled for a long time.

Lacey's assessment was close to the mark. Tucker and Dora talked at length about their writings and the involvement with the forthcoming newsletter venture. That bolstered their dangling insecurity. To be needed and to be able to draw upon one's skills to effectuate a sound purpose can be powerful medicine.

In the confines of her room, Dora could almost imagine herself back at the time when she threw herself into the joyful task of writing her column. There was research, interviews with probing questions, and numerous drafts until she was completely satisfied that she was conveying exactly what she wanted readers to glean from the words and thoughts. Just to anticipate capturing some of that was more than a reason to live. It was a cause to celebrate.

Tucker must have felt the same way because he invited Dora into his room to have a drink of bourbon from a small bottle he had secreted in on his arrival. Alcohol was forbidden at the home, and it was on the prohibited list by his doctor. Yet, it just seemed like a ripe moment for a toast. To regain a modicum of usefulness was to revisit his absorbing past, to catch and hold on to a memory of a better time. What was it that Carol said how Stanley used to describe it? Ah yes, that was it — to have glimpses of forgotten dreams.

The two enlivened oldsters had a nip using the paper cups in the bathroom for water. That certainly did not detract from the occasion, and they went on to chat as two old friends might. A mutual passion for writing would be a firm foundation on which to create a friendship. They went to dinner together and sat next to each other, their table companions duly noting the fresh animation of the newcomers.

It just seemed natural after that for them to be together at meals. The gossip soon raised the inevitable question — had the Stanley and Lauren magic emerged again?

Carol had the only computer at the home. Lacey was going to bring a laptop for the duo to use on her next visit, and in the meantime she sent updates to Carol who printed them out.

Tucker and Dora spent a good part of their days browsing through Carol's collection of professional books. They would point out germane sections to each other, and they took copious notes not quite sure yet what the first topic of the intended informative article would be.

It was during a visit to the home library that Dora met and befriended Violet. Violet spent a couple of hours a day in the library, mainly staring at Stanley and Lauren's books and wishing she could turn back the clock.

Dora entered the library to see what books were there. Upon seeing Violet, she smiled and extended her hand. "Hello. I am Dora."

Violet grasped the extended hand. "I know. I'm Violet, volunteer librarian."

"Ah, that sounds like a responsible undertaking."

"A very satisfying one. I take special care of the collection of books that were Stanley and Lauren's. Lauren and I were best friends."

"You both were lucky. Having a best friend is one of the most rewarding aspects of life. My sister was my best friend, and when I lost her a part of me went also."

"That's exactly how I feel. I am proud of the books but I cry almost every time I come in here because they symbolize her absence. I can talk to the books but they do not answer me."

"Would you mind if I look around?"

"No, please do."

Dora noted that none of the volumes in the library would be useful in a research quest. They were evidently geared for light reading. She read the sign below the collection of Stanley and Lauren's books, and pulled out a few and flipped through the pages. "You can tell much about people by their books. These are the giants of literature. Hopefully, I can make time later on to dive into them."

"Fine. I'll help whenever you need it."

"That is very nice of you. I bet Lauren appreciated the special person you are."

"I like to think so. She did so much more for me than I could have done for her. I'm just an ordinary person."

"Nonsense. No one is ordinary. We are all special in our own way."

Violet could not hold back. "Can we be friends?"

"We already are."

SIXTEEN

It was days later when Penny finally had an evening to herself. Between trips, she luxuriated in a hot bath. Later, sitting on the sofa and sipping from a glass of wine, she pulled Stanley and Lauren's treasure chest close to her on the coffee table. She lifted up the lid, feeling ever so close to her aunt as she envisioned that wonderful woman going through these same motions. Reaching in the quaint trunk, she pulled out a sheet of paper from the mass of papers and cards comprising the stored inventory.

Flattered with promise of escape
From every hurtful blast,
Spring takes, O sprightly May! Thy shape
Her loveliest and her last.

Less fair is summer riding high
In fierce solstice power,
Less fair than when a lenient sky
Brings on her parting hour.

When earth repays with golden sheaves
The labours of the plough,
And ripening fruits and forest leaves
All brighten on the bough;

What pensive beauty autumn shows,
Before she hears the sound
Of winter rushing in, to close
The emblematic round!

Such be our Spring, our Summer such;
So may our Autumn blend
With hoary Winter, and Life touch,
Through heaven-born hope, her end!

Thought on the Seasons
William Wordsworth

On the back of the sheet was another Wordsworth gem.

> *Instructed that true knowledge leads to*
>   *love;*
> *True dignity abides with him alone*
> *Who, in the silent hour on inward thought,*
> *Can still suspect, and still revere himself,*
> *In lowliness of heart.*

> Lines –
> Left upon a seat of a
> yew tree

The intellectual stimulation led her mind to wander. She was planning to go to *Mountain Splendor* and meet with Tucker and Dora, and she wanted to again impress upon Carol that there was so much good she could do on a far wider basis through LAURSTAN. Drawn together by their emotional association with Stanley and Lauren, and feeling confident and comfortable with Carol's abilities and motivation, a working friendship would be beneficial.

Selfish thoughts then took over. Not getting any younger, there could not be too much of a delay in having a family. To have a child to be close to and share the growing years, just as she recalled the closeness with her mother, was a dream vital for her future. The love of her life had been elusive. When she was a drug representative, she had hoped she might come across an eligible doctor who would catch her fancy. There just never seemed to be any opportunity to depart from business relations. None of the men she met were attracted to her, and she was not impressed by any of them.

Recently, she had met several male nursing home administrators. Several of them fell within an eligible category. Yet, there just was not a physical or emotional spark leading to stimulation as inducement to develop anything closer. Meeting a man to love and who would love her could very well be a more arduous task than completing an avowed and permanent success for LAURSTAN.

Helen Finch was involved in a different thought pattern concerning men. Her living arrangement with Fred had always been a strain as they seemed to exist on different life plateaus. It had taken a turn for the worse since he had been fired from his building job. Carpenters, once in high demand, had found rough going in a slacked-off construction environment, particularly when cheaper immigrant labor was available and could perform many of the building functions. Factory constructed home sections also did not help. He had encouraged Helen to change jobs not so much to support her desires but as a way of knowing she would be gone most of the day and would not nag him about finding work and to stop drinking.

Helen was now making the mortgage payments on the modest suburban home titled in her name, and it was a silent sacrifice. Taking public transportation to her job at LAURSTAN was an additional burden she had to bear. Fortunately, she loved her new job although she sorely missed the hands-on care for the elderly. Fred could never understand why anyone would want to care for withering old folks. According to him, they smelled badly and babbled nonsense. Lacking in him was any sensitive and caring nature that Helen possessed.

Finally, their life together hit a tortuous roadblock. Fred left to live with his brother in Seattle. Helen did not realize what a relief it was until he was gone. It had been energy draining and time-consuming trying to be a companion to an uncaring person who would rather drink than help a person in need. Her mother, who had died after a long illness, had described Helen as a person with a sweet soul. Caring for her mother during that protracted period had thrust her into life's role. It had been a major contentment knowing that she had prolonged her mother's life and had alleviated some of her suffering. Easing the transition to death was very rewarding.

As it turned out, Penny was not able to get out to the home as planned. She had been asked to speak at a conference in Chicago, and that event and its preparation forced her to back off from the visit. She sent Helen in her place, wanting Carol to meet her and to be conversant with all of the LAURSTAN staff. It was thought to be a good idea to have Tucker and Dora meet Helen as another avenue of communication with the organization.

Helen was quite impressed with *Mountain Splendor*. Her jobs at other homes had given her a good base to make comparisons. This was a place well run and where the welfare of the inhabitants was paramount. She could appreciate that and admired Carol for her strong and passionate leadership. The two women chatted for a long time, and the conversation was enjoyable.

Helen was also enthralled by Tucker and Dora. She was first introduced to them at lunch as Carol's guest. They talked afterwards as they sat on the rockers on the front porch. Helen was so impressed with the lively conversation and lucid thinking by the two oldsters, by the time she was to leave she felt close to them. An earnest hug was given to each, and Helen hoped Penny would send her back soon for another visit.

After Helen left, Tucker and Dora stayed rocking in the chairs on the porch. A comfortable silence permeated their closeness. After awhile, Tucker spoke first. "I like Helen. One of the many benefits of long years of experience with all sorts of people is that it becomes easy to recognize a genuine person."

"I agree. Of course, I see those same qualities in you, and I am sorry for you that many did not recognize and appreciate you for what you are. I am glad for many reasons to be involved with LAURSTAN."

"I see those in you as well. In a strange way, and it does sound odd for an old foggy to say it, I almost feel as if I have been reborn."

"It does not sound strange to me," and as if on impulse she reached for his hand and their fingers intertwined. "In fact, it sounds as wonderful as I feel."

The contact of hands touching was magical. Tucker could not recall the last time he held a woman's hand. It was such a natural and pleasing act. For Dora, it was the same kind of thrill she felt at age eleven when Kenny Hascal gave her the first kiss on the lips. It was remarkable she could feel such a rush of emotion when the slowness of old age had nearly smothered everything else. Radiating from the clasp of hands was a beguiling union of hearts.

Their first kiss came later that day when they finished the last of the smuggled liquor. Tucker gently brought her close to him and their aged lips met, the dryness dissipating in sweet nectar of meaningful togetherness. For the very first time in his life, just as the sun was about to set on his being, Tucker could honestly admit that he was in love.

Dora's marriage had eased her acceptance of love into her life as she had lived with it in all of its glory all of those years. She never thought she would or could feel that way again. Now, the emotion was not only recaptured it was escalated beyond any dreamed of expectation.

Later that night they joined in a supreme act of love. To their mutual surprise, their fading bodies responded to sexual urges long suppressed and believed to be forever dormant. They held onto the moment as they grasped to the call of their bodies.

Tucker planted fervent kisses all along her sagging body, oblivious to any imperfections. It was far more thrilling than the younger women he had in his distant past. For him, the secret of love is that it forgives the lack of beauty and fading perfection. It is an idea that lives and while gaining a special freshness it furnishes all of the glory that life can furnish.

Contrary to Stanley and Lauren's tact, these two decided to be extra careful that no one should know of their love. There would be no fanfare, no public spectacle. Private feelings would be kept that way. Any togetherness would appear to others solely to be for the writing and the other purposes of LAURSTAN. For a pair of elderly writers, it was a major thrill and captivating to have a secret love. The remaining pages of their book of life would be turned gingerly, one at a time, and each word and concept savored. There was no doubt that the final chapter would be the best.

SEVENTEEN

Even though they wanted their relationship to be different from Stanley and Lauren's, similar patterns developed. After breakfast, when the weather was accommodating, they would walk to the bench on the mountains side of the property where the ashes of the legendary lovers were scattered. The beauty of the spot and the quietness were captivating. Dora had to lean more and more on Tucker to negotiate the distance. The weaker her body became the stronger her love for Tucker emerged.

At times they talked about a myriad of subjects, each contributing an opinion or experience to enrich the conversation. At other times, they would sit in silence, even dozing, fingers intertwined.

Their favorite time was in bed, attempting to cuddle as closely as possible. They would be playful when Dora's energy prompted it, peaceful at those times when her body demanded a quiet interlude.

The future was a day at a time. Dreams were short-term and still vivid, and no less poignant than those of young lovers who believe the world is theirs forever. An old love is special because it holds no rash promises of extreme pleasures or outlandish results. It focuses on the here and now. Tucker and Dora, two rational and intelligent people, recognized the wonderful emotion they were living through. Not a thought would be cast that the curtain might descend at any moment.

Dora looked back at her marriage to a good man, lasting fifty-three years until his death, as a rewarding part of her life. To have now found another good man placed her in the ranks of the few really lucky women. Throw in a career she enjoyed and that was stimulating, and her life could only rightly be described as full and rich.

Tucker, in hindsight, termed his indiscretions and failure to commit as learning blocks for this extraordinary time and emotional crescendo with Dora. The experiences were a prelude to his one masterpiece of life. At age eighty-one, he had finally matured. At long last, he was dictating to life rather than the swings of life governing his way. A personal victory can be meaningful at any age. It is particularly sweet at the senior level.

Another entertaining and engrossing activity was reading the newspaper together. The newspaper would be spread out on the carpeted floor, and they would sit by it reading items aloud. Comments and quips were fast and furious, belying the so-called stultification of ancient minds. Some articles they would mercilessly pick apart; others would be commended for style and content. An intellectual game is an enchantment at any age.

It was easier to keep their loving relationship private than they had anticipated. Carol was so engrossed in busier involvements to take notice, and the other residents accepted the togetherness of the oldsters as necessary for the projects they were working on. There was no reason to look beyond what was apparent. Any tidbits of conversation overheard were far from personal and no signs of familiarity existed. It might have taken a master sleuth to unravel the façade. None of the residents fit into that category.

Even Violet had not a clue the two were deeply in love. She sought Dora's company as an offshoot of their new friendship, and if Tucker was around he silently left to do other things. Violet would spill her heart out to Dora, and she was comforted by the placid tone and sage counsel offered. Violet's health issues were becoming major and she expressed a fear of dying. Dora calmly exclaimed that she was not afraid to die. Accepting death is not any different than taking other things in stride. Life can have many twists and turns, and the secret to not letting them derail you is to meet them directly and dealing with them on their own terms. Death is final only if one deems it to be. She was not spiritual and was at peace with death as a final event in life. She encouraged Violet to seek a religious avenue if it would ease the way. So many do, and it can be most comforting.

Violet once again deemed herself fortunate to have become Dora's friend. A friend can tie up the loose ends, make sense out of sordid impulses, and the sharing of good and bad thoughts can be the great equalizer.

As the two women hugged, Violet was reminded of Lauren's weak embraces. She readily dismissed that impression basking in Dora's strength of composure and character. The true secret in finding good is wanting to feel good.

EIGHTEEN

It was during one of the nursing school classes that Lacey had a brilliant idea. Knowing her dear father deserved female companionship, and being so enamored with Penny, it would be wonderful if she could match the two of them together. Her father agreed to have Penny over for dinner, thinking nothing of it than that Lacey wanted her boss to meet him and to repay the kindness that had been extended to her.

As Owen waited for Penny to arrive, he could hear Lacey in the kitchen preparing the meal. His mind shifted to his long absent wife. Her abandoning the family was an act of cruel disloyalty. He had always been faithful to her, even though it had been difficult at times. He had not been attracted to any of his students so that had never been an issue. There had been a neighbor down the hall that he had romantic leanings toward when Lacey was still young. He had sensed that she was thinking in ways about him too. Shelly had a husband and a daughter just about Lacey's age. The two mothers exchanged babysitting when the need arose. If it was in an evening when Shelly would sit for Lacey, Owen always walked her back to her door even though it was just down the hall. They would walk close to one another and there were accidental bumpings. They would hug at her door and he sensed a subtle invitation in the way she would press her body into his. Yet, he never did pursue any overtures and acted at all times as the perfect gentleman. Shelly and her family moved away before Owen's wife left, and on some nights as Owen lay in bed trying to sleep he would see Shelly's face before him and have the sensation of her body pressed close to him. Memories can be warm and inviting. They can also be troublesome when they represent regrets for opportunities wasted. Pondering over regrets is futile although it can ease travel on later unmarked difficult pathways.

Shortly after arriving for dinner, it became apparent to Penny that Lacey was trying to match her up with her father. Penny thought that was very sweet, and it was totally in character with Lacey as a gently giving person. Owen was an interesting man, and the father-daughter relationship evidently warm and close, but there was no special attraction that Penny felt towards him. Owen never even arrived at a thought that Penny might be a women for him to be with. It was just a pleasant time with flowing conversation. Lacey, of course, was disappointed as she could tell the hoped for attraction did not materialize. Penny would remain a mother figure. It would be just in a different context.

The following week, Penny did get a chance to visit at *Mountain Splendor*. She took Helen with her as the lively talk about the place and of Tucker and Dora was nearly non-stop. Every time she would drive there she would think of the trip when she took her Aunt Lauren there. It seemed as if it was yesterday.

Penny and Helen chatted extensively with Carol in her office, and then they met Tucker and Dora at the lunch table. Penny gave them a briefing paper that Lacey had prepared detailing the happenings of the organization, and it was decided that the events part of the newsletter would be followed by a researched piece, a form of essay, on the rights of the elderly. It might have been easier for Lacey to do the first part but Penny wanted the two oldsters to feel as much a part of the organization as possible.

From all she had heard, Penny was predisposed to like the two oldsters. Helen and Lacey had raved about them. Carol had even spouted their virtues. They were easy to be with and the talk was animated. Dora seemed pale and her eyes dark, and Penny thought she might always be that way, but it did painfully raise her aunt's final days in her mind. The two made an interesting couple, and Helen was extremely attentive to the conversation.

Penny could appreciate that Helen had a special gift in dealing with old people. Carol also recognized this, and she privately asked Penny if she would mind giving her up. With the increased applications at the home and the newfound notoriety, the Board of Directors had approved a position of a resident assistant. Helen would be perfect for the job. Penny thought it was a wonderful idea, and she still had some resumes of qualified persons at her end. She would miss Helen but just knew that Helen would jump at this kind of opportunity.

Helen did not hesitate for a second. To be a resident administrator's assistant and to be available constantly as a caregiver was a dream come true. She put her house on the market and planned to sell whatever furnishings the house buyer did not want.

The room was small but that mattered not. After moving in, Carol introduced Helen around and then asked Violet to show her the layout of the place. Violet was happy to do this, and she referred to herself thereafter as the assistant's assistant. Violet was also now into making signs as she was proud of herself for the one she placed in the library for Stanley and Lauren's books. So, when she was showing Helen the clocks in Carol's office and telling her the story behind them, she placed a sign she had just made on the shelf besides the clocks.

> *These clocks belonged to Henry Hubbell.*
> *His stay at Mountain Splendor was cruelly short*
> *but through his clocks his presence continues.*
> *It is always his time.*

> *"No one knows when the clock of life will click*
> *away the final second of Life, and Death cometh.*
> *For the clock of life is wound only once."*

> From "The Clock" by
> Jackie Compton

Tucker had been spending more time in the library. He was entranced by Stanley and Lauren's books, particularly the old Cambridge Edition of the Great Poets. Henry Wadsworth Longfellow had always been a favorite, and on each visit he would pull that volume from the shelf and leaf through this master's works.

That night with aged body molded to aged body, he suggested to Dora that they use an excerpt from Longfellow in the first essay. "He has a beautiful way of saying what we believe needs to be said. Why not imbue the article with some added culture?"

Her response was to hug him as tightly as her waning strength would allow. She had never felt so tired. She gently caressed his cheek, hardly able to feel the stubble of the beard appearing long after his early morning shave. The sensation of touch in her fingers was fleeting, and she knew she was failing in so many ways. In the darkness of the room, illuminated only from a distant light in the parking lot, shadows were undefined and growing. Did he notice her weakening? She considered telling him but did not want to detract from the mood of the moment even if she could speak.

Love can recognize subtleties that others cannot see. Tucker grimaced realizing that the one true love in his life was gradually leaving his fervent grasp. He had rarely been able to hold on to the meaningful things in his life, and this too was slipping away. He kissed her lightly and his fingers moved slowly and gently along her body, all of the new discoveries and fresh memories seeping into his own body.

In the morning before Tucker informed Carol of Dora's passing during the night, he struggled to put her nightgown on. They would all know the two were sleeping together, but he wanted Dora to have the dignity of being clothed when the body was viewed.

Carol, Helen and Violet arrived to comfort Tucker. The realization was touching that here was another love that would continue to live in the heart. They all hugged, tears once again transporting the reality of an ending. Sad endings are heavy burdens that need to be shared.

By clutching on to the love and the memory, Tucker gained greater resolve and purpose. He finished the first LAURSTAN newsletter by himself. After a recital in the form of news flashes of the Director's trips and accomplishments as well as the status of staff projects, Tucker penned the first essay.

In the inaugural issue of the LAURSTAN newsletter, this is the first essay dealing with old people. It has a special purpose and meaning. The general theme will be discussions of the elderly, particularly who they are and what they represent to a society that does not appreciate them and fully care to or want to understand them.

It is written by two old oldsters, defined by sources as those over the age of eighty, who are residents of Mountain Splendor. One of these oldsters has passed away before the completion of this writing. That passing accentuates the reasons and importance of the truths aired in this forum. In addition to a tribute to all old people, these articles are dedicated to this sweet and loving person who left a trail of goodness in her life. She was a kind and gentle woman, a role model for all humanity. She was the kind of person you would want as a best friend. She will be remembered by those whose lives she touched. Farewell, dearest angel of the heart!

The most important aspect of an aging society is that the elderly know who they are, what they have done, and what they can do. The words of W. Somerset Maughm say it most elegantly. "The complete life, the perfect pattern, includes old age as well as youth and maturity. The beauty of the morning and the radiance of noon are good, but it would be a silly person who drew the curtains and turned on the light in order to shut out the tranquility of the evening. Old age has its pleasures, which, though different, are not less than the pleasures of youth."

Future articles will go into the existing legislation, both federal and state, geared towards affording the elderly rights and protection, as well as the international documents of the same nature. This is considered a worldwide issue. Proposed initiatives will also be examined.

This introductory writing will take a different tact, more of a philosophical approach. It is the opinion of the authors of this newsletter that the real tragedy is that such efforts are needed at all. By designating protection for the elderly and affording them rights means they are a class of people that needs them. All people are and should be treated the same, and just because they may have some differences by designating specific rights for them it is creating a classification giving credence to the argument that they are in fact different from other people. Old people are the same as young or middle age people. Old people have identical needs and aspire to the same wants. When one is old, one does not cease to dream. By classifying a group of humanity as old automatically recognizes and validates the belief that differences in fact exist. Human rights and civil rights apply to all. It is even a shame that such blanket rights need to be spelled out. It may sound trite but on a realistic level there are old persons who are younger than those who have not accumulated as many chronological years. The bottom line is that aging does not make one any less human, less worthwhile, less capable and deserving of enjoying the fruits of life's harvest. One may be older but should not be labeled derogatorily as old. Realistically, laws are needed to regulate persons and places that try to abuse or take advantage of any person, be they prisons, schools, or nursing homes. That is the sorry defect of human nature. The pity of it all is this is the way it is.

Humanity has been blessed at all ages with creative genius. One of the great poets, Henry Wadsworth Longfellow, offered this verse:

Enjoy the Spring of Love and Youth,
*   To some good angel leave the rest;*
For Time will teach thee soon the truth,
*   There are no birds in last year's nest!*

*   and –*

Be still, sad heart! and cease repining;
Behind the clouds is the sun still shining;
Thy fate is the common fate of all,
Into each life some rain must fall,
*   Some days must be dark and dreary.*

NINETEEN

Dora was buried next to her sister in plots in Maine the two had purchased when they were living together. Helen borrowed Carol's car and drove Tucker up to the burial site. It took two hours, and when they arrived they were the only two people there for the internment. A warm sun and a gentle breeze enveloped the scene, and Helen sobbed and tears trickled down Tucker's face. He had said his goodbye to Dora the night she died. Whispering in an ear, he pronounced his abiding love and the promise to carry her in his heart until his last breath. Now, in his mind a line from Longfellow sounded: *Great is the art of beginning, but greater the art is of ending.*

The gravediggers filled the dirt over the coffin and left. Helen grasped Tucker's arm as her symbol of sympathy. There were no words that could match the somber mood of the moment.

They rode back in silence, just as they had on the way there. Silence can be the greatest respect among people who care for one another. Silence can often absorb sadness better than vocal expressions.

Tucker would go on, catapulted by the brief love he knew, and he vowed to be his best in everything undertaken until his departure time. His remaining days would be dedicated to Dora. All of his accomplishments would be for both of them.

Helen knew that in her new position death would be a constant haunt. She accepted that as a necessary aspect of helping those in the waning years of their lives. Never to become complacent about it was the key. Supplying care and comfort for those precious moments was her driving force. She would also keep a special caring eye on Tucker. She marveled at his staunch bearing and his superior intellect.

Penny and Lacey felt Dora's loss deeply, and after finding out about the love she shared with Tucker, they felt so sad for him. They expressed their feelings to him on the telephone. His essay was wonderful, and upon discovering his preoccupation with Longfellow, they sent him a leather-bound volume of that giant's works so that Tucker might keep it in his room. That kind of thoughtfulness brought an additional tear to the old man's eyes.

It did not take long for Penny to find a suitable replacement for Helen on her staff. Phyllis Halpern, at age fort-five had already experienced much of life's mishaps and vagaries. At the top of her class in nursing school, she went to work for one of the largest and most prestigious nursing homes in the nation. After ten years, she rose to head nurse where she supervised the nursing staff. That brilliant career was cut short when a pick-up truck went through a stop sign and collided forcefully with her car. Paralyzed from the waist down she was relegated to spend the rest of her life in a wheelchair. That tragic event turned her entire existence on end. The nursing home job became an impossibility, and her weak and distant husband soon left her as he could not take the pressure of having to deal with an invalid. Well-meaning friends tried to be of assistance and to be the nurturer for a while but soon gave up as the daunting task detracted from their own lives. Her parents were deceased and her one brother was absorbed in his own complicated life. A hefty court settlement helped her to buy a small house and have it renovated to accommodate her disability, as well as to purchase a vehicle that was wheelchair accessible. She hired an orderly on the nursing home staff, James, to drive her on a part time basis as there were few places to go. Meanwhile, her fragile emotional bearing disintegrated and nothing brought any satisfaction. Boredom and lack of self-worth ruled her days. Self-pity is an erosion of the spirit. A momentary glimmer arose when Penny initially interviewed her. She was interested in the organization and felt strongly she could contribute greatly to its prospects. The disappointment of not getting hired was alleviated by the secondary offer that came when Helen left. The salary was unimportant. Her spirits were buoyed. She immediately enticed her orderly friend to leave the nursing home and to be her full time chauffer to take her to and from work, and then to help with chores around the house. It is amazing what a purpose in life can do for the disposition and outlook. Her easy and natural smile of earlier days returned immediately.

Phyllis and Lacey became fast friends. The youngster was easy to work with, and her bubbly personality further bolstered the mature woman's determination.

One afternoon Owen had to pick up some documents downtown so he stopped in to visit his daughter at the office. He also had some interesting news for Penny, although he did not know she was away on one of her assessment trips.

His visit prompted fireworks. Lacey introduced him to Phyllis, and her strong resemblance to Shelly, the neighbor from bygone days that he had such a strong attraction to, sent an emotional shock wave through his system. It was as if a past regret had rushed in as a second-chance to be righted. Her disability mattered not.

Phyllis was attracted to him as well.   Now, as if she had been able to sit back and appraise the world anew, this change in her existence left an opening for romance. Thinking no man would be attracted to a cripple, Owen's immediate attentiveness made it obvious that there was an interest. He seemed so much stronger and well meaning compared to the man she had married at an early age and which had turned out to be a loveless marriage. Lacey could not miss this fascinating development, and she smiled to herself as she went into Penny's office to work to leave the two of them alone to talk.

They conversed for over an hour, and the polite and continuous discussion merely confirmed that they wanted to see more of each other. Phyllis invited him for dinner on Saturday night, assuring him cooking was a simple matter in her specially designed kitchen. It was a date both would eagerly anticipate.

Before Owen left, he wrote a note to Penny and left it on her desk. He had no idea what that note would precipitate.

> *Penny –*
> *At a faculty meeting yesterday, I learned that a teacher is*
> *going to be hired for the fall semester for Rights of the*
> *Elderly. They asked if anyone knew possible candidates.*
> *I immediately thought of you and mentioned your*
> *credentials. It sparked an interest. If this sounds*
> *appealing, call Dr. Nugent at the college administrative*
> *office. The number should be in the telephone book.*
> *Good luck – and happy hunting.*
>
> *Owen*

Two days later, Penny arrived back from her trip. It was mid-afternoon by the time she opened the door to the office. She read the note, a wry smile coming to her lips. She lifted the telephone receiver and punched in Carol's number.

"Hello."

"Hello, future professor."

"Oh, how do I know some spectacular news is coming?"

"Correction. Present psychic and future professor."

"Cordiality aside, what's cooking?"

"Here it is in a nutshell. Lacey's father, Owen, has informed me that there will be a new course to be taught at the college in the fall on the elderly. He thought I might be interested, but you, dear friend, are so much more eminently qualified. If you jump at it and grab hold of this golden opportunity, it probably means you coming down here to teach for a day, you can stay with me and also work a day or two or three at LAURSTAN. Helen can handle everything from there for you, and you can guide her by telephone if necessary."

"You have my life all planned out," Carol spoke jovially.

"It's a natural. I still think we are destined to be the dynamic team removing the darkness surrounding old folks. Here is a perfect chance to see if I am right."

"This is rather sudden."

"As I said, it is not until fall."

"I'll think about it."

"Don't take too long. Others will be interested and competition might become fierce. I looked up the number. Call Dr. Nugent at the administrative office of the college. He'll give you the particulars. I am sure Lacey can ask Owen to put in a good word about you. 497-8727."

"Are you sure you don't sell used cars in the evenings? I bet doctors ordered drugs through you that they really didn't want or need."

"I need and want you here at LAURSTAN. Plain and simple."

"You are quite a person."

"No, you are."

After hanging up, Penny had a really good feeling that this was all going to work out. When Lacey told her about Owen and Phyllis, that just seemed to confirm the positive direction of events. They were all overdue for some bright moments in their lives.

TWENTY

Without a doubt, one of the cruelest and saddest events is if a child dies before the parent does. This was one of the emotional burdens that Albert Bellows had to endure. A ninety-one year old is not hardened to emotional shockwaves and any devastating attribute can, in fact, be even more difficult to bear at an advanced age.

His life had been a long one, and as with many other lives it was a composite of both good and bad. He would gladly have accepted an earlier death if his daughter could have been granted a longer stay in the world. At least his wife had not lived long enough to witness that tragic occurrence. She would have been totally broken-hearted.

As he sat back in his newly acquired room at *Mountain Splendor*, it seemed like a very long time ago when he had met his wife. It was during his first job as a file clerk at a large insurance company. Maureen was a typist in the typing pool, along with several dozen other women. Rumors ran amuck about these ladies, ranging from sedate tales to wild portrayals of feminine antics. Most of the men had nothing to speak of about her. The word was that she was so sensitive as to disdain men completely. That overrode her plain looks as far as he was concerned. He had always been attracted to a sensitive woman as he was sensitive himself, a trait no doubt inherited from his overly sensitive mother. The typing pool was located on a floor with few offices, and the typists occupied open desks spaced close together. He would have to be creative to make an official trip to that floor, but whenever he did he would stare right at her and was usually rewarded by a smile. Working up courage, he finally asked her to join him for lunch in the lunchroom. They started dating, and a year later married. She worked on to put him through law school. After he passed the bar examination and was admitted to practice he found a job at a small law office. Maureen stopped working just before their first and only child was born.

Pamela was another sensitive addition to the family. Eventually she also became a lawyer and built a career at the firm at which her father was by then a full partner.

Life was comfortable and stable until Maureen was diagnosed with cancer and died a month before they would have celebrated fifty-four years of marriage. Albert had been retired for ten years, and before Maureen's illness they traveled extensively.

Pamela never did marry, perhaps because her sensitivity and contrasting career drive left little room for possible suitors. After Maureen's death, Albert moved in with Pamela and she tended to whatever increasing care he needed as old age took its toll and slowed him down. Pamela's cancer was not detected early enough even though she had regular examinations because of the family medical history. Albert was the one who cared for her. Her painful demise stultified whatever spirit he had, and while still able to care for himself on a personal level, he could not live alone. He had seen the documentary on *Mountain Splendor* awhile back and noted that if and when such a need arose that would be the kind of place to spend his remaining days.

It just so happened that Dora's death left an opening that none on the waiting list could immediately act on. So, he found himself ensconced in Dora and Lauren's room. Carol had assured him that no one would intentionally intrude on his peaceful moments but that he might find solace in many others there who also had confronted an array of life's emotional and physical downturns.

Carol introduced him to Tucker, his next door neighbor, and the two men developed a quick and endearing friendship. Stories of Maureen and of Dora paved the way for many open and personal discussions.

One afternoon as a warm late summer breeze came down the mountains, the two men sat on rockers on the front porch. Tucker recalled sitting there and holding Dora's hand. It lifted a lid on his emotions. "I often wish I could relive the past. I have a series of regrets that should be undone."

> *Regret, that little good hath marked,*
> *Our years forever fled.*
> *Regret, for graves within the heart,*
> *Where vanished hopes lie dead.*

> Regret
> Fannie May Gibbes

The older man blinked a couple of times. "You cannot turn back the clock."

"I know that. It just seems we ought to have a chance to right a wrong."

"Mother Nature and Father Time brought you to this point. I dare say everyone has regrets. Not being perfect, we cannot live a perfect life. The secret is not to dwell on the mishaps of the past. We need to concentrate on the positives. I am relearning that now as I rock in this chair and getting nowhere. What you gave Dora certainly compensates for what you did or withheld in the past."

Tucker was silent for a moment. "Regrets can be thought of in terms of curiosity. If we did a thing differently, it may have turned a life in a new direction."

Albert snickered. "Or, it may have turned out worse. You do not know, and never will know. People get hung up on remembering what failed or deprived us of some happiness or success. When we look back it appears as a disaster. Perhaps it was, but the fact that you are around to tell the tale means more. For all we know, it could have turned out more hurtful and we might not even be around to feel sorry for ourselves."

"You have regrets, I am sure."

"Ah, yes. Yet, life is a roller coaster ride. For all of the downs there are the ups. A number of regrets are matched by the instances where a pat on the back is deserved." Lost in his own thoughts for a few minutes, he then resumed speaking. "The important thing is that the past is gone and the future may never come. The here and now is quite enough to deal with. At our age each day is a gift, a precious span of time that needs to be nourished and guarded. Do not look back, and do not look ahead. Now is on our plate and demands all of our attention."

"Don't you feel you need to look forward to something?"

"Testing my wisdom, aren't you? Well, my friend, I look forward to any chance to make today better than yesterday and not as good as tomorrow, if there is a tomorrow. Loneliness is the true regret of today. I miss my wife and daughter."

"I miss Dora. We were just on the verge of sharing so much. In a wisp it was gone, like a puff of smoke carried off in the wind. Now, our time together is just a secret anniversary of the heart."

"That's what young people fail to grasp. A precious moment, a meaningful relationship, a personal emotional reward can be gone so quickly. Rather than merely accepting it, effort is needed to perpetuate it. They tune out that kind of reality and let life dictate consequences to them rather than fashioning life to a significant result. In a way it is too bad we learn such an important lesson late in life."

"Yes, and that is the other sad fact. Young people have ears of stone when an oldster tries to impart experience and wisdom. I was guilty of that myself. It is compounded when the cycle keeps repeating itself."

Nearly in unison the two men dozed off, haunting dreams to prevail until awakened to a demanding moment. The breeze had stopped and the air was still as if it was trying to absorb the lessons of the conversation. Or, was it all just a reflection of the young when the sage advice just vanishes into thin air?

Back in his room, Tucker opened the Longfellow volume. He knew that his description of his time with Dora as secret anniversaries of the heart was from a Longfellow poem.

> *The holiest of all holidays are those*
>> *Kept by ourselves in silence and apart;*
>> *The secret anniversaries of the heart,*
>> *When the full river of feeling over-*
>>> *flows; —*
> *The happy days unclouded to their close;*
>> *The sudden joys that out of darkness*
>>> *start*
>> *As flames from ashes; swift desires that*
>>> *dart*
>> *Like swallows singing down each wind*
>>> *that blows!*
> *White as the gleam of a receding sail,*
>> *White as a cloud that floats and fades in*
>>> *air,*
>> *White as the whitest lily on a stream,*
> *These tender memories are; — a fairy tale*
>> *Of some enchanted land we know not*
>>> *where,*
>> *But lovely as a landscape in a dream.*

Holidays

TWENTY-ONE

James was happy to do all of the shopping for Phyllis to prepare the dinner for Owen. He had admired her capable and mature leadership at the retirement home, and was so saddened by the accident. It meant the loss of a respected boss and he feared then the loss of a good friend. When she offered him the part-time job of chauffeuring her around and then the full time job to do other chores concerning the house, he felt lucky. As much as he enjoyed the work at the home, he did not hesitate in accepting this opportunity. Living in a small apartment close by with his young and pregnant wife, Corinne, was a benefit. He knew he would have to find a larger living space once the baby arrived. It elated him to finally see Phyllis happy.

Unaccustomed to being nervous, Phyllis moved around in her wheel chair in the specially equipped and adapted kitchen more than she probably had to. Entertaining a man, a special man, was new and exciting for her. It had to be just right. This might be her last chance to capture love and to approach a normal life. Never believing that a man would love her in this condition, there was no way she was going to let this chance slip away.

The lemon sauce and fresh cut dill on the salmon filled the house with a sensual aroma. The pants of the suit covered her motionless legs, and the fitted jacket conformed to her small frame. The straight brown hair fell to her shoulders, and for an instant she believed she could be beautiful. The navigation of the wheel chair took on ease as opposed to the chore it was most of the time. Perception can often affect routine and temperament.

Owen was nervous too as he arrived at the house. He had gone beyond the initial attraction based on her resemblance to Shelly. He had gone over and over in his mind the extended conversation they had and her bright and animated participation. On reflection, there was a softness about her mannerism, and it was evident that her strength of character had emerged victorious over adversities.

All of this was confirmed over a long evening of quiet conversation at the dinner table and then in the sitting room. He helped her out of the wheel chair to sit next to him on the sofa. His touch pleased her, and her fresh fragrance and warm skin renewed his male drive so long left fallow by inaction. They kissed tenderly and then again with more urgency. The rising passion left little doubt that a love of major proportions was brewing. Life, a mystery of sorts, adds to the allure as people can go from a form of inertia to a venture filled with far-flung exciting vistas.

This was the same evening in which Penny found herself relaxing at home for the first time in quite awhile. The greatest form of solitary comfort had become reading passages from the treasure chest. She sat back on the couch and stared at the trunk feeling a binding force with her Aunt Lauren that easily emanated out to encompass all of the old people who might be in horrible places or frightened with no one to look after them with concern and love, waiting and perhaps wishing for death to free them.

Penny stuck her hand deep into the trunk, sheets of paper, index cards and cutout articles and book pages engulfing her hand. They made her hand warm and that warmth drifted towards her heart. Scraping the bottom, a thin sheet of paper beckoned to be lifted out and read.

Sometimes a breath floats by me,
An odor from Dreamland sent,
That makes the ghost seen nigh me
Of a splendor that came and went,
Of a life lived somewhere, I know not
In what diviner sphere,
Of memories that stay not and go not,
Like music heard once by an ear
That cannot forget or reclaim it,
A something so shy, it would shame it
To make it a show,
A something too vague, could I name it,
For others to know,
As if I had lived it or dreamed it,
As if I had acted or schemed it,
Long ago!

In the Twilight
James Russell Lowell

The comforting beauty of the words and the concepts, brought on a thirst for more. Again, the hand entered the storehouse of beauty, ruffled through the paper mass, and emerged clutching another gem to enjoy and ponder over.

When I compare
What I have lost with what I have gained,
What I have missed with what attained,
Little room do I find for pride.

I am aware
How many days have been idly spent;
How like an arrow the good intent
Has fallen short or been turned aside.

But who shall dare
To measure loss and gain in this wise?
Defeat may be victory in disguise;
The lowest ebb is the turn of the tide.

Loss and Gain
Henry Wadsworth Longfellow

Sleep was especially peaceful that night. A mind saturated with beauty is calmly invigorated, stimulated not to wakefulness but to a tranquility fostering contented rest. She had a dream about Aunt Lauren. She was commending Penny for her noble efforts. Even in dreams, Aunt Lauren was inspiring just as she had been all of her life. Especially was the case in the culmination of a life filled with achievements for others producing a personal harvest. Her mother and aunt would definitely be proud of her. She was proud of herself.

Carol had several telephone conversations with Dr. Nugent. The teaching position sounded perfect for her. It would be a chance to convey her expertise combined with true life experiences. Perhaps it would inspire some of the students to seek careers in the field. It was also tempting to join Penny in the practical crusade to advance the embattled cause for old people. Yet, her heartstrings tugged her in a different direction.

There were two prolonged visits to Stanley and Lauren's bench where in that tranquil setting she mulled over the choices. After the second venture, she returned to her office and stared at Stanley's hat and Henry's clocks. It became clear that as enticing as the opportunity might be, and as much as entering a broader and more active life style might increase the chance of finding romance, she just would not be able to tear herself away from this place. The people, her family, were housed in her heart. It would be a form of abandonment to leave them. Helen had confirmed the significance of the hands-on care and concern so vitally needed for a caregiver. An opportunity like this might never come along again but this life was her calling and her destiny.

Penny was disappointed to hear of this decision but knew that Carol had thought it over carefully. She respected her too much to persuade her otherwise after such a deliberation. Dr. Nugent urged her to reconsider and offered to keep her resume close at hand.

The memory of Stanley, Lauren, Henry, Dora and so many others whose final days were carved in her soul solidified the decision. It was a relief to reaffirm she was where she wanted to be. Doing good on a small scale also plays an important role in the development and progress of humanity. Small rewards can be as enriching as grandiose achievements.

TWENTY-TWO

"Even a blind squirrel comes across a nut once and awhile," Albert pronounced at the next porch discussion with Tucker.

The two men looked forward to these talks. There were no great solutions offered for the world's problems. Yet, it was uplifting to wax prophetic. Eliciting challenging remarks and partaking in self-philosophy honed over many years of experience are satisfying in their own way.

Tucker could not restrain himself. "Don't say everything that is in your mind or show all that is in your wallet."

"James Russell Lowell said only by unlearning does wisdom come."

"That must make me very wise. As with Mark Twain, each day I forget more than I ever learned."

"And, the most important advice of all, do not fully listen to the disjointed ramblings of two old men." They laughed, and the moment was golden. Yet, golden moments do not last long.

They were silent as the siren was heard in the distance. Muscles tensed as the foreboding sound became louder as the ambulance approached and stopped with a sharp braking sound before the front door of the home.

They stared at the front door as the paramedics rolled out the gurney. A dejected sigh involuntarily passed through Tucker's lips. It was Violet. She had been found unconscious in her room.

Carol and Helen were close behind. Carol got in the ambulance and it sped away with the siren eerily at full blast. Helen seeing Tucker sitting close by came to him and reached for his hand. Helen knew that Tucker and Violet were close as a result of Dora's friendship with her. "We'll go to visit her at the hospital as soon as we are allowed."

In response, Tucker squeezed her hand. If only Dora had lived longer not only to enjoy the bountiful love he had to offer her but also to bask in the kindness of the people surrounding them. Age is no barrier to finding a new life.

Sadly, as it turned out, there would be no visits at the hospital. Violet never did emerge from unconsciousness and had died shortly after arriving at the emergency room. The excessive weight was too taxing on an already strained heart.

When Carol had first returned from the hospital witnessing Violet's death she had been physically and emotionally exhausted. She stared at

Henry's clocks and Stanley's hat. She was soothed by the ticking of the clocks and her will reinforced by the constancy of the swinging pendulums. The captain's hat represented the far and wide capture of the imagination and the spirit. Once again, her decision was solidified. The inner satisfaction of being with the people who trusted her at the time of their greatest need could not be replicated elsewhere. Even though unconscious, Carol never let go of Violet's hand until the doctors declared her dead. Somehow Carol believed that Violet knew she was there. Violet had not died alone.

While clearing the personal effects from Violet's room, Helen found a sheet of paper on the desk next to a volume on Tennyson from Stanley's collection that Violet had borrowed from the library. Did Violet know that her life was about to end? The writing, printed neatly in pen, sure seemed to indicate such an outlook.

> *But in my spirit will I dwell,*
> *And dream my dream, and hold it true;*
> *For tho' my lips may breathe adieu,*
> *I cannot think the thing farewell.*

Death may not be the end of sad events. An informal memorial service was held for Violet at the home. Many of the residents attended. From Violet's address book filled with the so-called friends she had known over the years, Carol had notified them of Violet's passing and the planned memorial service. Not a single one showed up. Not a one even sent flowers or a note of condolence. Such is a depressing commentary on the significance of past associations.

At the service, Carol spoke affectionately of a woman who in loneliness emerged strong and confident by a meaningful friendship with Lauren and Dora. That led to her active helpfulness to others and the home, notably her care of the books in the library and the signs she made. She then read the Tennyson quote found in Violet's room. Soft sobbing could be heard throughout the assembly.

Tucker then brought the entire gathering to tears as he described a life cut far too short when a heart still had meaningful deeds to perform. Her passing meant that they all needed to complete her dreams. He then read one of his favorite Longfellow poems, a portion of which he had put in the essay for LAURSTAN.

The day is cold, and dark, and dreary;
It rains, and the wind is never weary;
The vine still clings to the mouldering
                        wall,
But at every gust the dead leaves fall,
            And the day is dark and dreary.

My life is cold, and dark, and dreary;
It rains, and the wind is never weary;
My thoughts still cling to the mouldering
                        Past,
But the hopes of youth fall thick in the
                        blast,
            And the days are dark and dreary.

Be still, sad heart! and cease repining;
Behind the clouds is the sun still shining;
Thy fate is the common fate of all,
Into each life some rain must fall,
            Some days must be dark and dreary.

TWENTY-THREE

The last leaves of autumn had fallen from the trees, and the cold winds were gusty in anticipation of winter's grip. Tucker and Albert moved their ranting sessions indoors, and these slowly evolved into the two men writing jointly for the LAURSTAN newsletter. They collaborated on a book delving into the not-so-real mysteries of old age entitled Passion and Compassion. Throughout her endeavors Penny had enlisted so many media members that she was able to get to a publisher for the two errant writers and get the book published. It was a slim volume with no wasted words or fluff to soften the message. Albert died before the first printing, and Tucker once again needed to overcome another void in his life. He was comforted by knowing that Albert had fulfilled T.S. Eliot's dictate: *Old men ought to be explorers.*

LAURSTAN was the leading customer for the book. Penny would give complementary copies on her speaking engagements and visits to other homes. It brought to brighter light her message and fortified proposed actions. Carol also kept a supply on hand to give to visitors and new arrivals. Tucker was a local hero and celebrity. The fame did not replace Dora or Albert although he accepted any plaudits on behalf of all of them.

Contemporaneously with the publication of the book, the wedding of Owen and Phyllis brought a welcomed happy event into all of their lives. The love that had developed between them had transgressed any physical impediments and the union was blessed for others being nourished by the beneficence of such an abiding love. Lacey moved into the house with them and a week later was given the dog she had always wanted. Phyllis had a cottage built behind the house for James and Corinne to live in with their newly born son, James, Jr. James continued to help with the domestic chores and worked at times at LAURSTAN to help out. Corinne also helped with matters as she could. All became fond of the baby and as he emerged as a lively and personable little one, they all looked on him as a son of their own. The sounds of a child's laughter enrich the closeness that fondness engenders.

Penny, Carol and Helen had sat together at the wedding. A bond of mutual respect held them in a meaningful union of their own. Penny and Carol could only hope that there might be a wedding of their own at some point. Yet, while it would be a greater fullness to their lives now, the sense of being useful and devoted to their design represented a certain completeness of their being. If a love was out there, they would attain it just as Lauren, Dora and Phyllis had. For Helen, the love of what she was doing obliterated the distaste of her bad relationship with Fred and was her fulfillment.

Tucker sat close to them but by himself. It was a pensive time, envisioning he and Dora as the groom and bride before him. Her loving memory would sustain him until that moment when he would draw his last breath. Until then, he would do all he could to uphold the cause that brought them together.

For once, the tears of the three women were of joy. For those who are truly caring, the happiness of others becomes their happiness. The fulfillment of the dreams of those they care about are a certain realization of their own dreams. Forgotten dreams are revisited and the earlier glimpses become a full panorama of living. Such is the lasting lesson learned from the lives of Stanley, Lauren, Henry, Violet, Albert and countless other elderly people who have overcome the stigma of old age to be who they wanted to be and meant to be without hesitation or restriction. True contentment comes in being just that way and with the interaction of others close at hand. Each breath drawn is a gift. Each kind and gentle act is a joy. Each moment of loving thoughts and actions is the essence of existence.

The book is completed.
And closed, like the day;
And the hand that has written it
Lays it away.

Dim grows its fancies;
Forgotten they lie;
Like coals in the ashes,
They darken and die,

Song sinks into silence,
The story is told,
The windows are darkened,
The hearth-stone is cold.

Darker and darker
The black shadows fall;
Sleep and oblivion
Reign over all.

Curfew
Henry Wadsworth Longfellow

***

Following are "glimpses" of earlier absorbing and compelling novels by the author which have not been "forgotten." In fact, they have been well received, and loyal readers eagerly anticipate publication of new intoxicating stories.

2001 - *In a World We Never Made* is a "scholarly novel." Set in a college in the early 1970s, some nonfiction is interjected into a spell-binding story of professors and students dealing with age-old problems of identity and desire. The work is replete with proverbs.

2003 - *A Door Never Opened* is a stand-alone sequel to the first novel. In a present day setting, some of the same main characters face substantial emotional issues without a total escape from their earlier lives. It is a celebration of living and loving. Some of the actual love poems that the author's father wrote to his mother are incorporated throughout the engrossing story.

2005 - *Shadow Selves* is a thoughtful tale of two idealistic young people who are outsiders from society. Through each other they learn to overcome their own inadequacies, to take on the battle of others, and they discover that love is the most powerful of binding forces. Original short stories by the author are included in the captivating events. These stories, as with the novel itself, carry deep and abiding lessons for living a meaningful life.

2006 - *Network of Death* is a gripping murder mystery. Puzzling ghastly torturing and murdering of high-priced call girls who service the convention trade through a secret network lead two homicide detectives on cold trails and to blocked ends. These same detectives also wrestle with critical personal conflicts. The twists and turns in this highly acclaimed mystery will keep a reader keenly engrossed as the plot unfurls.

2008 - *Not Lost — Just Not Found* is about a university psychologist dealing with an assortment of clients striving to identify and pursue happiness and who have fascinating stories to tell. While guiding others, he finds that he is the ultimate test of his own philosophy. Readers will certainly empathize with the host of characters.

2009 - *Restless Beauty* is a truly unique work. It is the engrossing story about a beautiful lake that is shrouded in mystery and reputed to have a restless spirit. For hundreds of years it has been the attributing factor for death, suffering and financial ruin for those who dare disturb it. Some people believe the lake can produce goodness. Threaded throughout are the feelings of six lonely people who are brought together by the lake.

www.timetreasuresbooks.com

* * *